Senior
Short.
Stories

# Writing from Scotland

# Figures in a Landscape

# Figures in a Landscape

## Writing from Scotland

Gordon Jarvie

CAMBRIDGE
UNIVERSITY PRESS

PUBLISHED BY THE PRESS SYNDICATE OF THE UNIVERSITY OF CAMBRIDGE
The Pitt Building, Trumpington Street, Cambridge CB2 1RP, United Kingdom

CAMBRIDGE UNIVERSITY PRESS
The Edinburgh Building, Cambridge CB2 2RU, United Kingdom
40 West 20th Street, New York, NY 10011–4211, USA
10 Stamford Road, Oakleigh, Melbourne 3166, Australia

First published 1997

Printed in the United Kingdom at the University Press, Cambridge

Typeset in 9.5/13.5 pt Sabon

*A catalogue record for this book is available from the British Library*
ISBN 0 521 57577 X (paperback)

Prepared for publication by Paren & Stacey Editorial Consultants
Formatted by The Wadsley Workshop
Cover photograph: Glenelg and Skye © D. Corrance

Senior Short Stories

MO10282

# Contents

# Acknowledgements

The editor and publishers wish to thank the following for permission to reproduce illustrations and photographs:

p.xvi Gunnie Moberg; p.4 The National Museums of Scotland, © The Trustees of the National Museums of Scotland, 1997; p.8 David Sim; p.20 The National Galleries of Scotland; p.28 The Scotsman and Gary Doak; p.32 The National Museums of Scotland, © The Trustees of the National Museums of Scotland, 1997; p.42 The Scotsman and Allan Milligan; pp.62–63 The Oscar Marzaroli Trust, © Anne Marzaroli; p.72 Douglas Corrance; p.78 The Oscar Marzaroli Trust, © Anne Marzaroli; p.96 Douglas Corrance; p.104 The Oscar Marzaroli Trust, © Anne Marzaroli; p.118 Cordelia Oliver; p.126 Colin McPherson

Thanks are also due to the following for permission to reproduce stories: p.1 John Murray (Publishers) Ltd for George Mackay Brown, 'Tartan' from *A Time to Keep*, 1969; p.7 Peters Fraser & Dunlop Group Ltd on behalf of the Estate of the author for Eric Linklater, 'The Duke' from *God Likes Them Plain*, Jonathan Cape, 1935; p.16 John Johnson Ltd on behalf of the author for Jessie Kesson, 'The Bridge' from *Where the Apple Ripens*, Chatto & Windus, 1985; p.21 Ian Hamilton Finlay for 'The Old Man and the Trout' from *The Seabed and Other Stories*, 1958; p.27 Curtis Brown Group Ltd on behalf of Mrs Sylvia Rhea Martin for Lewis Grassic Gibbon, 'Clay' from *A Scots Hairst*, Hutchinson, 1967. Copyright © Lewis Grassic Gibbon; p.44 Gordon Wright Publishing Ltd on behalf of the author for David Toulmin, 'Touch and Go!' from *Hard Shining Corn*, Impulse, 1972; p.50 Chambers Harrap Publishers Ltd for Naomi Mitchison, 'A Matter of Behaviour' from *A Girl Must Live*, Chambers, 1990; p.57 HarperCollins Publishers for Brian McCabe, 'The Face' from *The Red Hog of Colima: Scottish Short Stories*, Collins, 1989; p.64 Gordon Jarvie Editorial on behalf of the Estate of the author for George Friel, 'A Couple of Old Bigots' from *A Friend of Humanity and Other Stories*, Polygon, 1992; p.71 David Higham Associates on behalf of the author for Joan Lingard, 'Silver Linings' from *Glad Rags*, Hamish Hamilton, 1988; p.79 Bess Ross for 'The Bit about Growing' included in *Shouting It Out*, ed. Tom Pow, Hodder Educational, 1995; p.89 The Calder Education Trust for Elspeth Davie, 'Sunday Class' from *The Spark and Other Stories*, John Calder, 1968; p.105 Polygon for James Kelman,

'Away in Airdrie' from *Not Not While the Giro*, 1983; p.129 Louise Turner for 'Busman's Holiday', first published in *Glasgow Herald*, 30th July 1988 and included in *Starfleet*, ed. Duncan Lunan, The Orkney Press, 1989.

This book is dedicated to Mike Hayhoe,
general editor of the
*Figures in a Landscape* series,
who died while it was in preparation.

# Introduction

An editor of a 'national' collection, like this one, has to warn that an in-depth, comprehensive, national collection cannot really be achieved within the covers of a single, smallish book. All you can try to do is pull in as many of the strands and complexities of a modern cultural landscape as possible. That is all I have attempted here. So it is – unavoidably and unashamedly – an anthology of *my* Scotland.

A few geographical comparisons to start with.

Like England, Scotland is a small country. Its land area is sixty per cent of the size of England, a shade smaller than Portugal, but bigger than the Republic of Ireland, Denmark, the Netherlands or Belgium. Its population is only ten per cent of England's, but about the same as Denmark's, more than Ireland's, but less than Portugal's, the Netherlands', or Belgium's.

Geographers often divide Scotland into three sections: the Highlands and Islands; the Southern Uplands; and in between these, the Central Belt. Ninety per cent of Scots live and work in the Central Belt, in and around cities like Glasgow, Edinburgh and Dundee. Travelling in the Highlands or Islands, or in the Southern Uplands, you often get the impression of a very empty country. Where are all the people? You can see that they were once there. Deserted buildings and hamlets can often be seen in the countryside. On winter days, when there is a light dusting of snow on the hillsides, you can sometimes pick out the lines of the old field systems – almost as you could if you were doing aerial photography. So you know that the country-side wasn't always as empty as it now is. Indeed many people have remarked at the 'lived-in' feeling you get, even in some deserted areas.

Over the past two hundred years, the Highlands especially have become one of the last great wildernesses of Europe. If you read the story called 'The Duke', by Eric Linklater, you'll learn a little about the Highland Clearances, one part of the explanation of today's empty countryside.

A wonderful feature of the great wildernesses of Scotland is the wealth and variety of their wildlife, from deer to salmon, to ospreys and golden eagles and many other threatened species. Stories like 'The Kitten' and 'The Old Man and the Trout' remind us that the Scots share their landscape with an unusually wide range of wildlife.

I said that ninety per cent of Scots live and work in the Central Belt. Sometimes this area is referred to as the Central Lowlands, which is a misnomer. The Highlands and the Southern Uplands may be more mountainous, but the Central Belt itself is also very hilly. The Ochils, Sidlaws, Campsies, Lomonds, Pentlands, Lammermoors, are the names of only a few of the substantial hill ranges in the so-called 'Lowlands'. So another feature of the Scottish landscape is its overall hilliness. Even the cities are hilly in aspect. What other European city has a vast volcanic sleeping lion in its midst like the great hill mass of Arthur's Seat in the middle of Edinburgh? Apart from this, and the famous Castle Rock, Edinburgh surrounds and runs up many hills – Corstorphine, Braid, Blackford, Calton – and has the Pentlands sweeping right to its doorstep. Glaswegians and Dundonians too have their hills, and the urban vistas provided by them. Scots may take their hills for granted, but visitors tend to remark on them and admire them.

The mention of visitors raises the topic of tourism, one of Scotland's key industries today. Many of the human figures in our landscape are tourists, even in the most out-of-the-way locations. I recently stayed with my family at an isolated bed-and-breakfast farmhouse on Orkney, where we woke to the sound of curlews and high winds and that special kind of island silence. The other guests at the farmhouse were intrepid American Midwesterners, on their first visit to Scotland. At the same time, there was a busload of East Europeans off a cruise ship 'doing' the island. And there were many cars with European number plates – Dutch, German, French.

A lot of visitors to Scotland, especially the transatlantic and antipodean ones, come in search of their roots. They often have surnames like Wallace or Kennedy, Affleck or Macdonald, Cameron or Campbell. Their ancestors may have emigrated, they may have been forcefully cleared off their land, they may have been transported to a penal colony for sheep-stealing or for wearing the kilt, or they may just have been part of a more recent brain-drain or economic movement. They are part of a large Scottish diaspora, sometimes more Scottish than the resident native Scots, often a little disappointed to find that the Scottish culture they're seeking is not more tangible and visible.

Weather is a feature of any landscape. Being farther north than England, Scotland has a cooler climate. Plants and crops ripen later than in the south of England. There is a noticeable difference in the light. Being nearer the North Pole and the 'land of the midnight sun', we have longer hours of daylight in summer (and shorter in winter). If you like the long, light nights, go to the north of Scotland. Lerwick, in Shetland, has 19 hours of daylight in June (London has only 15). Conversely, Lerwick only has six hours of daylight in December to London's eight.

As well as an interesting geography, Scotland's landscape also has a rich and well-documented human history. It is one of the oldest nations in Europe, and the two opening stories in this collection – 'Tartan' and 'The Duke' – are taken from this long history.

In terms of language, Scotland's cultural landscape has three main strands today – Scots, English and Gaelic. It is only recently that schools have started to respond positively and creatively to the use of Scots. Not so long ago, many people treated Scots as a form of 'bad' English, and school-children were punished for using it – myself included. Schools are now beginning to recognise that Scots is a rich sister language of English; it is in fact the 'mither' tongue of a majority of Scottish school students, so it is coming to be seen as something to be developed rather than discouraged by the schools. In this collection, the stories 'Clay' and 'Touch and Go!' in particular are written in versions of modern Scots. Several other stories draw more or less heavily on Scots vocabulary.

Any visitor puzzling over an Ordnance Survey map today will be aware of Gaelic place names in the Scottish landscape, especially in the Highlands and Islands. Gaelic has been spoken in Scotland for longer than any other known language. It reached Argyll from Ireland in the fourth century AD, and had absorbed the Pictish culture and tongue of northern Scotland – to which it was related – by the ninth century. It also overwhelmed the Norse language of the Viking invaders of Scotland's west coast, and was at its peak in Scotland between the ninth and thirteenth centuries. It has always been strongest in the north and west of the country. Gaelic is spoken today by only 66,000 people (less than two per cent of Scots), mainly in the Outer Hebrides, Skye and Lochalsh. Words of Gaelic crop up in various stories in this collection, including especially 'The Bit about Growing', 'The Man in the Boat', and 'The Man in the Lochan'. All Gaelic terms are glossed at the back of the book.

The languages used in this collection also reflect the social variety in the Scottish cultural landscape, from Standard English and middle-class Scots, to the colloquial, or demotic, varieties of working-class language, most notably the Glaswegian Scots of the housing schemes around that city, and the broad, Doric tongue of rural Aberdeenshire and the north-east.

The social and linguistic strands of the Scottish cultural landscape have obvious echoes in the Scottish literary landscape. A powerful strand of Scottish writing deals with the supernatural. This can be traced right back to the Border ballads and to classic texts like 'Tam o' Shanter' by Robert Burns or 'The Tale of Tod Lapraik' by Robert Louis Stevenson. Look at 'The Man in the Boat' and 'The Man in the Lochan' for modern examples in this collection. Another strand of contemporary Scottish literature, currently powerful, can be described as working-class realism; 'A Couple of Old Bigots' and 'Away in Airdrie' are examples of this type of writing.

A word about stereotypes: Scotland and the Scots are as raddled with them as any other country. I have tried to keep out of their way in this collection. Thus, couthy and sentimental stories of the school of 'Dr Finlay' and 'High Road' have been left out. There are no visuals of kilted bagpipers, or of stags at bay on the road to the Isles. I don't want to convey images of that sort of glossily sanitised, formica-covered Themepark Scotland; you can get these any day on your TV screens or at a cinema near you. As I said at the beginning of this Introduction, my Scotland is a highly complex, mainly urban, post-industrial society. Stories from coalmining communities, especially where the pit has been shut down, seem to me a particularly authentic detail in today's Scottish landscape. Stories like 'The Face', 'The Cure', and 'A Couple of Old Bigots' are set in such locations.

Anthologies like this book are samplers. They are convenient present-ations of a wider range of material than can normally be assembled within the covers of a single book. I do hope you will enjoy this sampling, and that you'll find at least two or three stories which say something important to you. That being the case, I hope the next thing you will do is to seek out more writing by the authors who particularly grab you.

*Gordon Jarvie,*
*Edinburgh*

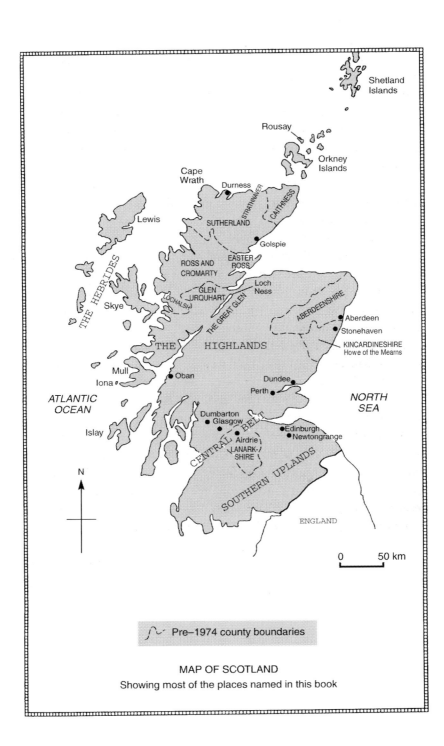

Shetland
Islands

Rousay

Orkney
Islands

Cape
Wrath
Durness

STRATHNAVER

CAITHNESS

SUTHERLAND

Golspie

Lewis

THE HEBRIDES

ROSS AND
CROMARTY

EASTER
ROSS

GLEN
URQUHART

Loch
Ness

LOCHALSH

Skye

THE GREAT GLEN

ABERDEENSHIRE

Aberdeen

Stonehaven

KINCARDINESHIRE
Howe of the Mearns

THE        HIGHLANDS

Mull

Oban

Dundee

Iona

Perth

ATLANTIC
OCEAN

NORTH
SEA

Dumbarton
Glasgow

Islay

CENTRAL BELT

Edinburgh
Newtongrange

Airdrie
LANARK-
SHIRE

SOUTHERN UPLANDS

N

ENGLAND

0        50 km

~ Pre–1974 county boundaries

MAP OF SCOTLAND
Showing most of the places named in this book

George Mackay Brown, 1921–1996 (Gunnie Moberg)

# Tartan

GEORGE MACKAY BROWN 1969

This modern story reminds us that Scottish writing comes from a very long continuum, in which Scottish history remains one of the inspirations.

'Tartan' is a story about the Vikings who, from the 9th century, came over the sea to Scotland in their longships looking for farmlands and fortunes. The author reminds us that the Norsemen were perhaps not all that different from us. Nor were they all savages: Olaf in this story is a poet and writer, one of the people who gave us the sagas which tell how life was long ago in the far north of Scotland.

Durness is on the north coast of Sutherland, not far from Cape Wrath. Rousay is one of the smaller and more fertile of the Orkney islands, and 10th-century Byzantine coins and a variety of Norse remains have been found there.

They anchored the *Eagle* off the rock, in shallow water, between the horns of a white sandy bay. It was a windy morning. Behind the bay stretched a valley of fertile farms.

'We will visit those houses,' said Arnor the helmsman. Olaf who was the skipper that voyage said he would bide on the ship. He had a poem to make about rounding Cape Wrath that would keep him busy.

Four of the Vikings – Arnor, Havard, Kol, Sven – waded ashore. They carried axes in their belts.

Gulls rose from the crag, circled, leaned away to the west.

The first house they came to was empty. But the door stood open. There was a shirt drying on the grass and a dog ran round them in wild noisy circles. Two sheep were tethered near the back wall.

'We will take the sheep as we return,' said Havard.

Between this house and the next house was a small burn running fast and turbid after the recent rain. One by one they leapt across it. Kol did not quite make the far bank and got his feet wet. 'No doubt somebody will pay for this,' he said.

'That was an unlucky thing to happen,' said Sven. 'Everything Kol has done this voyage has been wrong.'

Another dog came at them silently from behind, a tooth grazed Arnor's thigh. Arnor's axe bit the dog to the backbone. The animal howled twice and died where he lay.

In the second house they found a fire burning and a pot of broth hanging over it by a hook. 'This smell makes my nostrils twitch,' said Sven. 'I am sick of the salted beef and raw fish that we eat on board the *Eagle*.'

They sat round the table and put the pot of soup in the centre. While they were supping it Sven raised his head and saw a girl with black hair and black eyes looking at them from the open door. He got to his feet, but by the time he reached the door the girl was three fields away.

They finished the pot of broth. 'I burnt my mouth,' said Kol.

There were some fine woollen blankets in a chest under the bed. 'Set them out,' said Arnor, 'they'll keep us warm at night on the sea.'

'They are not drinking people in this valley,' said Havard, who was turning everything upside down looking for ale.

They crossed a field to the third house, a hovel. From the door they heard muttering and sighing inside. 'There's breath in this house,' said Kol. He leapt into the middle of the floor with a loud berserk yell, but it might have been a fly buzzing in the window for all the attention the old woman paid to him. 'Ah,' she was singing over the sheeted dead child on the bed, 'I thought to see you a shepherd on Morven, or maybe a fisherman poaching salmon at the mouth of the Naver. Or maybe you would be a man with lucky acres and the people would come from far and near to buy your corn. Or you might have been a holy priest at the seven altars of the west.'

There was a candle burning at the child's head and a cross lay on his breast, tangled in his cold fingers.

Arnor, Havard and Sven crossed themselves in the door. Kol slunk out like an old dog.

They took nothing from that house but trudged uphill to a neat grey house built into the sheer brae.

At the cairn across the valley, a mile away, a group of plaided men stood watching them.

At the fourth door a voice called to them to come in. A thin man was standing beside a loom with a half-made web in it.

'Strangers from the sea,' he said, 'you are welcome. You have the salt in your throats and I ask you to accept ale from Malcolm the weaver.'

They stood round the door and Malcolm the weaver poured horns of ale for each of them.

'This is passable ale,' said Havard. 'If it had been sour, Malcolm the weaver, we would have stretched you alive on your loom. We would have woven the thread of eternity through you.'

Malcolm the weaver laughed.

'What is the name of this place?' said Arnor.

'It is called Durness,' said Malcolm the weaver. 'They are good people here, except for the man who lives in the tall house beyond the cairn. His name is Duncan, and he will not pay me for the cloth I wove for him last winter, so that he and his wife and his snovelly-nosed children could have coats when the snow came.'

'On account of the average quality of your ale, we will settle matters with this Duncan,' said Arnor. 'Now we need our cups filled again.'

They stayed at Malcolm the weaver's house for an hour or more, and when they got up to go Kol staggered against the door. 'Doubtless somebody will pay for this,' he said thickly.

They took with them a web of cloth without asking leave of Malcolm. It was a grey cloth of fine quality and it had a thick green stripe and a thin brown stripe cutting across it horizontally. It was the kind of Celtic weave they call tartan.

'Take it, take it by all means,' said Malcolm the weaver.

'We were going to take it in any case,' said Sven.

'Tell us,' said Havard from the door, 'who is the girl in Durness with black hair and black eyes and a cleft chin?'

'Her name is Morag,' said Malcolm the weaver, 'and she is the wife of John the shepherd. John has been on the hill all week with the new lambs. I think she is lonely.'

'She makes good soup,' said Arnor. 'And if I could get hold of her for an hour I would cure her loneliness.'

It took them some time to get to the house of Duncan because they had to support Kol who was drunk. Finally they stretched him out along the lee wall of the house. 'A great many people will suffer,' said Kol, and began to snore.

The Gaelic men were still standing beside the cairn, a good distance off, and now the girl with black hair had joined them. They watched the three Vikings going in at the fifth door.

Ivory chess pieces from the Isle of Lewis, carved by Viking craftsmen over 800 years ago

In Duncan's house were three half-grown children, two boys and a girl. 'Where is the purchaser of coats?' said Havard. 'Where is the ruination of poor weavers? Where is Duncan your father?'

'When the Viking ship came into the bay,' said a boy with fair hair, the oldest of the children, 'he took the mare from the stable and put our mother behind him on the mare's back and rode off south to visit his cousin Donald in Lairg.'

'What will you three do when we burn this house down?' said Arnor.

'We will stand outside,' said the boy, 'and we will be warm first and afterwards we will be cold.'

'And when we take away the coats for which Malcolm the weaver has not been paid?' said Arnor.

'Then we will be colder than ever,' said the boy.

'It is a clever child,' said Sven, 'that will doubtless utter much wisdom in the councils of Caithness in a few years' time. Such an orator should not go cold in his youth.'

They gave the children a silver Byzantine coin from their crusade the previous summer and left the house.

They found Kol where they had left him, at the wall, but he was dead. Someone had cut his throat with a corn-hook.

'Now we should destroy the valley,' said Havard.

'No,' said Arnor, 'for I'm heavy with the weaver's drink and it's getting dark and I don't want sickles in my beard. And besides all that the world is well rid of a fool.'

They walked down to the house where the sheep were tethered. Now eight dark figures, including Malcolm the weaver and Morag and the clever-tongued boy (Duncan's son), followed them all the way, keeping to the other side of the ridge. The men were armed with knives and sickles and hayforks. The moon was beginning to rise over the Caithness hills.

They killed the two sheep and carried them down the beach on their backs. The full moon was opening and shutting on the sea like the Chinese silk-and-ivory fan that Sven had brought home from Byzantium.

They had a good deal of trouble getting those awkward burdens of wool and mutton on board the *Eagle*.

'Where is Kol?' said Olaf the skipper.

'In a ditch with his throat cut,' said Sven. 'He was fortunate in that he died drunk.'

The Durness people stood silent on the beach, a score of them, and the old bereaved woman raised her hand against them in silent malediction.

The sail fluttered and the blades dipped and rose through lucent musical rings.

'The poem has two good lines out of seven,' said Olaf. 'I will work on it when I get home to Rousay.'

He steered the *Eagle* into the Pentland Firth.

Off Stroma he said, 'The tartan will go to Ingerd in Westray. Kol kept her a tattered trull all her days, but with this cloth she will be a stylish widow for a winter or two.'

# The Duke

ERIC LINKLATER 1935

The now notorious Highland Clearances provide the background for this story. The Clearances began after the failure of the 1745 rebellion, and lasted over a century. During that period, vast tracts of the Highlands and Islands were 'cleared' of their people, many of whom starved or were forced to seek new lives overseas. The cleared countryside was then given over by the landowners – often the aristocracy – to profitable sheep-farming and game-hunting. Thus the Clearances were an early example of what has more recently and chillingly been termed ethnic cleansing.

'The Duke' is set towards the end of this terrible time, and the references to the Crimean War (1854–6) give the exact period in which the story is set. The Duke of Sutherland, one of the arch-clearers, expects 'his' people to accept his patriotism and pride and go off to fight for Queen and Country. But this elegiac, angry tale shows that the ordinary people of Sutherland have their own agenda, and their own pride.

Standing inhumanly tall, on the hill called Ben Bhragie, was the statue to the old Duke. It was a monument to crime, a memorial to greed and folly. In his name and by his authority the happiness of a broad countryside had been laid in ruins, and misery domesticated. Many thousands of people had been robbed of land that was theirs by the right of immemorial usage, and evicted with every circumstance of brutality from the homes their fathers had built and they had plenished. Leaving behind them a blazing roof, carrying what they could of their small wealth, encumbered by the aged and the weak and by crying children, the stricken Highlanders had been driven from their native valleys like refugees before a barbaric invader. Yet no foreign power was hostile to them. Their enemy was their own chieftain. In nine years fifteen thousand of them had been turned out of their snug inland farms and exiled on a barren coast where, from weedy rocks and a sour turf, they might compete for a starved living with coneys and gulls and harsh weather.

Had they been savage and debased, their fate would still have been pitiful. Had their hills been the home of bandits, their villages of corruption,

Statue of George Granville Leveson-Gower, 1st Duke of Sutherland, on the hill called Ben Bhragie (David Sim)

such punishment might still be thought severe. But they had been, on the contrary, a people given equally to virtue and to valour. Peaceful in their private lives, as soldiers serving their chieftain or their king they had been famous for their audacity in attack, for the sternness of their courage in adversity. On their farms they had lived in quiet simplicity, in the field – in France and on the Peninsula – they had won for the Ninety-Third Highlanders a glory more proud than Roman eagles. They had deserved well of all men, even of their enemies, and their enemies indeed remembered them with respect. But their chieftain had betrayed them because they owned land that he coveted. That was their crime. They tilled their farms, and lived on the product of their toil, but he, who was already a leviathan of wealth, made little or no profit out of them. Sheep would pay him better. So he told his agents to drive them out, and bring flockmasters from the south to replace them. That was why his statue was raised so inhumanly tall on Ben Bhragie.

The Castle was set pleasantly among fields. Planted with trees, they were acquiring the mellow and accomplished appearance of a nobleman's park. The Castle was square, with towers at the corners, but preparations were being made to enlarge it, to add a wing, another tower, and a massive and ornate front. Foundations were being dug for the wing, piles of timber and cut stones were lying about, when the Duke – the son of the statued Duke, and himself now old – came north from London with a duty to discharge. Britain was at war with Russia, and the Queen's army needed men for the Crimea. The Duke was a patriot, and he had promised to recruit some hundreds of his own clansmen. The offer was warmly welcomed by Her Majesty's ministers, for no finer fighting men could be found, and the Duke assured them that they would soon have another battalion to throw against the Russian redoubts.

Hurried preparations for a great recruiting meeting were made in Golspie, a village on the coast, a mile or two south of the Castle, and notices were sent round the neighbouring parishes to warn people of the Duke's presence and apprise them of their duty to attend. These orders were respectfully received, and on the morning appointed at least four hundred men assembled in Golspie, at a place where the street broadened and where two recruiting sergeants were already walking up and down. Tables had been set on trestles, and there were chairs behind them, including a hand-some leather-furnished armchair for the Duke. The crowd regarded these arrangements without much apparent emotion. They were quiet and well-behaved, talking together in little groups, and gradually coalescing into a closely packed throng as more and more late-comers arrived, and the pressure grew of women and children on the flanks of the assemblage. These were more inclined to be noisy, calling shrilly to each other in Gaelic, till their menfolk sternly bade them be quiet. Absolute silence lay on the crowd when the Duke arrived.

He came in a carriage drawn by a pair of fine grey horses. His factor was with him, there was an officer wearing long Dundreary whiskers, and a minister of the Church of Scotland who had served his patron well by telling the crofters that eviction from their holdings was an act ordained by God, as a just punishment for their sins, and they must suffer it patiently and without resentment. Other members of the Duke's household, clerks and underfactors, had already arrived, and the recruiting party arranged itself behind the trestle-tables, a sergeant on either flank and the Duke enthroned in the middle.

They became busy with certain matters preliminary to the enlistment of the clansmen. Pens and ink-bottles were set out, piles of attestation papers laid on the table. The factor produced a black leather bag from which he took several fat bundles of pound-notes securely fastened, and arranged them so that they could be clearly seen. Then he undid a linen bag and poured from it, into a plate on the table, a glittering stream of sovereigns. He whispered a little joke to the minister, who sat beside him, but the minister held up a warning hand, for he saw that the Duke was ready to speak.

The Duke rose slowly, thrusting himself up from the arms of his chair. His voice was husky to begin with. The words, though confident enough, came haltingly. But he gathered strength, and soon was talking with some volubility.

'We are confronted with a crisis of great magnitude,' he said, 'and I have come here, as representative of Her Majesty and as your chieftain, to ask you all, or as many of you as may be able, to help our country, our great country of which we are so proud, in this her hour of need. The situation, with which you are all familiar, is this: we have taken up arms on behalf of a weak country, whose cause is *right*, against a great and powerful country whose only title to consideration is *might*. We are at war with Russia, whose tyrannous and despotic government is a menace to the freedom and independence of every country in Europe. We are fighting on the side of Turkey, because Turkey stands for honour and justice and civilisation and progress. It is essentially a Christian war in which we are engaged. It is a war that will help to rid the world of the recurrent menace of war. Her Majesty, and Her Majesty's ministers, and all of us here today, are lovers of peace, but only of an honourable peace. We would rather die – if necessary – on the field of battle, than live in a state of dishonourable ease, knowing we had abandoned what was right and forfeited the respect and friendship of our Turkish allies. I ask you to enlist, for this just war, in your own regiment, the Ninety-Third Highlanders, whose splendid reputation, known all over the world, was made by the courage and devotion to duty of your fathers and grandfathers. Or if, for any particular reason, you want to join some other regiment, you are at perfect liberty to do so. I may say, however, that my factor will pay the sum of six pounds, over and above the government bounty, to every man who joins the Ninety-Third, or a sum of three pounds to anyone who prefers to join another regiment. This money I am giving, and giving gladly, out of my own purse, as a stimulus to recruiting and because in times like these it behoves all of us to do what we can – though some of you, I know, cannot do very much – in the common cause. Now Major Hatton will read to you the terms of enlistment, and after that the sergeants, or the clerks here, will be ready to take your names. And I hope there will be a very good response to my appeal, and that Golspie will set an example to the whole country.'

For a few seconds the Duke remained standing, waiting for the applause that was his due. But no cheering rewarded him, no clapping of hands. The crowd, almost motionless, stood in absolute silence. Even the children were quiet. The recruiting party, embarrassed, shuffled in their chairs. The Duke, with brittle coughing, cleared his throat and sat down.

A moment later Major Hatton rose and read, in a dry precise voice, the terms of enlistment. 'Those of you who intend to join Her Majesty's forces, and I hope that includes nearly all of you, can now give your names either to Sergeant Murray or to Sergeant Rose,' he concluded.

There was no movement in the crowd, none came forward, no one shouted a question. They stood elbow to elbow, pressed close together, their faces void of any expression but mild expectancy. They looked steadily at the Duke and his party, waiting with gentle curiosity for the next exhortation, the next move.

The Duke's factor got up and said bluffly, 'Come, now, who'll be the first? Who's going to show the way and set the pace? What about you, Ross? Or you, Murdo? Wouldn't you like to feel six golden sovereigns in your hand?'

He took a fistful of gold and poured it from one hand to the other. 'Who's going to take advantage of His Grace's marvellous generosity?' he demanded.

There was no reply. A little shuffling movement went through the crowd, and then they settled again to immobility and silence. The recruiting party began to confer in anxious tones, and the sergeants, obeying Major Hatton's order, went forward to talk with individuals in the throng.

The crowd, as though shaking itself, opened its ranks a little to let the sergeants in. Their red tunics disappeared in the dull hued mass, their feather bonnets shook and wandered above four hundred heads. No hostility was shown them, but whenever they spoke to a man he shrugged his shoulders or turned his back. One of them came out with a shock-headed squinting fellow, who seemed a volunteer, but there was a good deal of laughter at his appearance, and the minister, hurrying forward, told the sergeant to let him go again, for he was the village idiot. Except for him the sergeants had no success.

Once more the Duke rose slowly and began to speak. His voice was angry now. He told them how serious was the situation, how urgently men were needed in the Crimea. He repeated most of his previous speech, referred again to his bounty, and trembling with indignation declared that their behaviour was such an insult as he had never in his life received. But he would give them one more chance. Who would join the colours? Who were not afraid to be men, and who were simply cowards?

The silence on the crowd seemed to grow more heavy. It lay on them like a roof, and beneath its weight they seemed to contract, to grow in upon themselves. They stood like men made of stone. Even the sound of their breathing was subdued.

The Duke still waited for a forward movement to break their ranks. But no movement came. Then in a passion he shouted, 'This is the first and only time in history when the men of Sutherland have refused a call to duty! Your fathers and your grandfathers would be ashamed to own you. They were heroes, and you are dastards. Whenever there was danger, wherever there was war, the Highlanders – your brave ancestors – were first against the foe.

And do you, their sons, hang back and hold to the skirts of your women-folk like poltroons? What are you frightened of? Of the enemy? Your fathers faced the world in arms. Are you frightened of getting hurt? You'll be well looked after if you're wounded. Your country will treat you generously and see that you never want. Great Britain doesn't forget those who serve her! Your wives and children will be properly cared for while you're away. I myself will make it my sacred charge to see that no one suffers the smallest hardship whose breadwinner is fighting his country's battles.'

Like a black ripple on the sea, a sound of bitter laughter ran through the crowd. It passed, and silence followed. It passed as quickly as a catspaw of wind, blowing down from the cliffs, will overrun a narrow bay. But brief and small as it was, it disconcerted the Duke, who sat down, heavily and suddenly, and gripped the arms of his chair, and stared at the crowd with some obscure emotion in his soul and in his eyes.

Then an old man came out from the heart of the crowd. It opened slowly, like a dark leaf opening, and he came out and stood in the open space between the men of Sutherland and the recruiting party. He stood straightly and firm on his feet, not a big man, but tall enough to have a look of authority, though his face was lined with sorrow and his eyes were the eyes of a man who had seen disaster more often than triumph. He took off his bonnet – it was old and faded – and spoke in a high clear voice, in the accents of one whose natural talk was the Gaelic, but in words that did not fail him though he had to put his thoughts into English.

'Your Grace,' he said. 'We are indeed the sons of our fathers who fought so often for their King, and fought so well that you and all men remember them with pride. We are their sons, I say, and because of that we remember their fate who trusted to your promises, and to the promises of your ances-tors. It was near this very place that your maternal grandmother, at forty-eight hours' notice, mustered fifteen hundred men and chose out of them the nine hundred she wanted for the King's service. And they went willingly, as volunteers, because they trusted her, and she would make, I am thinking, the same promises that you have made. But what did they find when they came home again, or when their few survivors came home? They found their fathers and their wives, their sisters and their children and the widows of their comrades, sitting desolate and hungry and homeless on the cold seashore, whom they had left in fine houses, with cattle about them and ploughed fields in the inland glens. They found the good land that was theirs a desolation, a wilderness in the hands of strangers, and no sound in the air but the bleating of sheep, where once they had heard the bagpipe and the clarsach and the women singing. That is what your promises are worth, and that is why they deceive us no longer, because we are wiser than our fathers! Here is Donald Ross, with the mark on his forehead where the blazing beam fell from the burning roof of his mother's house, when your factor drove them out! There is John MacDonald, who lived, he and his family, on a diet of boiled grass and limpets for three long years, because he had been robbed of the farm that was his fathers' farm for six hundred years; and his four men children died of hunger and cold. If you had left them on their land they would have lived, and they would have been the Queen's soldiers, and every man of them might have killed ten Russians apiece! But they are dead, and you cannot enlist them now, though you offer sixty pounds a head for them. Nor will their father go at your command, and for your promise, because he knows what your promise is worth and what your bounty is like. You say the Czar of Russia is a tyrant and a despot, and that may well be the truth. But we in Sutherland say this, that if the Czar of Russia took possession of Dunrobin Castle and of Stafford House next term, we would not expect worse treatment at his hands than we have had at the hands of you and your family for the last fifty years. So go back to Her Majesty and tell her that you have found no men for her service, because you and your servants have driven them away from their hills and their glens, and the few that remain among the ruins and the rubbish of the county will no longer listen to your lying words. Go back to Her Majesty, and say that you have no men left in your land, but if she wants venison or mutton she can have it in plenty. For it was sheep and deer that you preferred to men, it is sheep that live on all the good land today, and sheep are all you can now command!'

Once or twice during this harangue the Duke had made an effort to interrupt and silence it. But words failed him, or the strength to speak them, and he sat, with a face as white as parchment, and twitching hands, till it came to an end. Then he rose abruptly, staggering against the table so that the sovereigns jingled in their plate, and walked unsteadily to his carriage. He looked at no one, neither at the old man who had spoken so daringly, nor at the men behind him, nor at his own people. His head was bent, his eyes saw nothing but the trodden earth before him. He would not wait for the others, but got into his carriage and was driven at once to the Castle.

Till he was out of sight the crowd was quiet enough. But when he had gone they began to grow more lively. The factor and the minister and Major Hatton were left with the tables to clear, and they hardly knew whether to clear them at once or to wait awhile to see if matters mended. But the factor prudently packed the money, the sovereigns and the pound notes, back into his bag, and made the two sergeants stand in front of him while he did so. Then there was a little laughter, and the children on the outskirts of the crowd began to imitate the bleating of sheep. The women followed suit, and some of the younger men. *Baa-a-a-a*, they cried, and laughed, and bleated again.

The minister tried to stop them, shouting angrily, but they bleated in concert, and the air was full of the silly noise of the flocks that had dispossessed them. They followed the recruiting party back to the Castle, baa-ing like shorn ewes. Their dignity was forgotten now, in which they had stood so long unmoved and silent, but they remembered how to laugh, and they saw that the years had given them reason to laugh, as well as to mourn. *Baa-a-a-a*, they cried. If the Duke and his hirelings preferred sheep to men, then they must like the foolish noise of sheep. They bleated again.

The flocks on the mountains heard them, and bleated too. Uneasy wethers carried the crying westward. It spread from Golspie to Lairg, and up Loch Shin. It crossed Ben More, and ran along the sides of Loch Assynt. It came to the Atlantic shore, so that over the whole country there was heard the sound of mockery. The south country shepherds in their bothies, nervous and ill at ease, called to their dogs. And in Dunrobin Castle the Duke stopped his ears with trembling hands. But he could not keep out the noise of his defeat.

# The Bridge

JESSIE KESSON 1985

'Belonging' is important for most people, especially when they are very young. Titch has to find out the hard way that belonging to a gang can involve a lot of painful learning. By 'spanning' the bridge, he has to prove himself to his slightly older peer group and demonstrate that he's not 'chicken'.

Jessie Kesson (1916–94) was almost seventy when she published this tale. Her insights into the pains of growing up are a reminder that older folk often understand the young very well indeed.

For the first time in his eight years, he had caught the biggest tiddler. A beezer it was. Even Mike – the tiddler champ – grudgingly admitted its superiority.

'But maybe it's the jam jar that makes it look so big,' Mike qualified.

'Some kinds of glass makes things look bigger.'

It *wasn't* the glass that made it look bigger. He had urged Mike to look inside the jam jar. And there swam surely – the king of tiddlers.

'*I* don't reckon it much.'

Anxious to keep on Mike's side, Titch McCabe peered into the jar. 'And Mungrel doesn't reckon it much either. Do you, Mung?'

Mungrel, who never spoke until somebody else put words into his mouth, agreed with Titch. 'S'right. I don't reckon it much neither.'

'Could easy not be a tiddler at *all*!'

Dave Lomax shouted from his perch on the branch of the tree. 'Could just be a trout. A wee trout!'

'– Could be . . .' Mung echoed; for although he had never set eyes on a trout he was in agreement with the others to 'disqualify' the tiddler.

'Let's *go* men!' Mike commanded. Suddenly tiring of the discussion.

'Scarper! First to reach the chain bridge is the *greatest*!'

'You're not some kind of wee trout.' He protested. Running to catch up with them.

'You're *not* . . .'

He stopped running to peer into his jam jar to reassure its occupant.

'You're a *tiddler*. And you're the *biggest* tiddler we've catched the day.'

'*Hold* it, men!' he shouted to the others. 'Wait for me.'

The authority in his voice surprised himself. Usually he was content enough to lag behind the others. Tolerated by them, because he was handy for doing all the things they didn't like to do themselves. Like swiping his big brother's fag ends. And ringing the bell of the school caretaker's door. Or handing over his pocket money to 'make up the odds' for a bottle of 'juice'. But *today* he was one of them. He had caught the biggest tiddler.

It was when he caught up with them at the bridge that his newly found feeling of triumph began to desert him.

'OK tiddler champ,' Mike said.

'Gi' us the jar. We'll guard the tiddler.'

'Yeah. Give,' Mung echoed.

'It's *your* turn to span the bridge,' Dave said.

He grasped his jar firmly against his anorak. He didn't need anybody to guard his tiddler. He didn't want to span the bridge either! *Nobody* spanned the bridge until they were *ten* at least! The others had never before expected *him* to span the bridge. He had always raced across it – the safe way – keeping guard over all the tiddlers while the others spanned it.

'*Your* turn,' Mike was insisting. '*We* have spanned it. Hundreds of times.'

'*Thousands* of times!' Dave amended.

'Even *Mungrel* spans it,' Titch reminded him. 'Don't you Mung? And Mungrel's even titchier than me!'

'Mungrel's *eleven*,' he pointed out. 'I'm not even nine yet.'

'Only . . . Mungrel's not *chicken*!' Mike said, 'Are you, Mung? You're not chicken.'

'I'm not chicken *neither*!' he protested. 'I'm *not* chicken.'

'OK! OK!' they said. Beginning to close in on him. 'OK! So you're not chicken! . . . *Prove* it . . . just prove it . . . that's *all*! Span the bridge and *prove* it.'

He knew how to span the bridge all right. Sometimes – sometimes kidding on that he was only 'mucking around' he practised a little. Spanning the part of the bridge that stood above the footpath. Knowing that even if he fell he would still be safe – safe as he felt *now*. Knowing that the ground was under his dangling legs.

Left hand over right – left over right – all his fear seemed to have gone into his hands. All his mind's urgings could scarcely get them to keep their grip of the girder.

Left over right – left over –

The river's bank was beneath him now. Dark pools flowed under the bank, he remembered. Pools where the tiddlers often hid – the *biggest* tiddlers. Sometimes he had caught them just sitting bent forward on the bank. Holding his jam jar between his legs. His bare feet scarcely touching the water. He'd felt afraid then, too. A *different* kind of fear. Not for himself. Just of things which his eyes couldn't see. But which his hands could feel. Things that brushed against them . . . Grasping and slimy.

He would never have been surprised, if, when he brought up his jam jar to examine its contents, he discovered neither tiddler nor tadpole inside it, but some strange creature, for which nobody had yet found a name.

Left over – right – left –

The shallows were beneath him now. Looking, even from this height, as safe as they had always looked. His *feet* had always told him how safe the shallows were. A safety – perfect in itself – because it was intensified by surrounding danger.

You could stand, he remembered, with one foot in the shallows, your toes curling round the small stones. While your other foot sank into the sand – down and down . . .

Left over right, left over right – over –

He had a feeling that his body would fall away from his arms and hands long before he reached the end of the bridge.

Left over right – over.

It might be easier that way. Easier just to drop down into the water. And leave his hands and arms clinging to the bridge. All by themselves.

Left over – right.

He was at the middle of the river now. That part of it which they said had no bottom. That could be *true*, he realised. Remembering how, when they skimmed their stones across the water, into the middle, the stones would disappear. But you could never hear them *sound* against the depths into which they fell.

Mike had once said that, though the water *looked* as quiet as anything – far down, where you couldn't see, it just kept whirling round, and round, waiting to suck anybody at all down inside it . . .

– over – right – left –

He wouldn't look down again. He wouldn't look down *once*. He would count up to fifty. The way he always counted to himself – when bad things were about to happen.

One two three four five six . . . Better to count in tens, he wouldn't lose his 'place' so easily that way –

One . . . two . . . three . . . four . . . five . . . six seven eight.

He thought he could hear the voices of the others. He must be past the middle of the bridge, now – the water beneath him was still black but he could see shapes within it.

The voices were coming nearer. He knew that they were *real*.

'CHARGE! MEN!' Mike was shouting. 'CHARGE!'

He could hear them reeshling up the river bank. And their feet clanking along the footpath. They were running away . . . Ever since he could remember the days had ended with them all running away. Only *this* time, his tiddler would be with them too. And Mike would boast that *he* had catched it. He had almost forgotten about the tiddler. And it no longer seemed to matter.

Green and safe, the bank lay below him. He could jump down now. But he wouldn't. Not yet! It was only titches like Mungrel, that leapt down from the girder, the moment they saw the bank beneath them.

Mike never did that. He could see, clear as anything in his mind's eye, how Mike always finished spanning the bridge, one hand clinging to the girder, the other gesturing, high, for a clear runway for himself before swooping down to earth again with cries of triumph!

'*Bat* Man! *Bat* Man!'

*A Hind's Daughter*, by James Guthrie, 1883

# The Old Man and the Trout

IAN HAMILTON FINLAY 1958

It is not only old people who can be wise. In this quiet and evocative tale, an adult recalls being eleven or twelve years of age, and learning about gentleness and about caring for wildlife and for other people. The story is very visual, which is not surprising in the work of a writer who has also been an active sculptor, artist, and landscape gardener.

He was tenant of a red-roofed cottage where we spent a summer holiday once. I suppose I must have been about eleven or twelve years old at the time. It was late on in the summer evenings the old man used to spin me his sleepy yarns. While he yarned we sat together on his wooden garden-bench, in view of his green and yellow honeysuckle bushes full of late-shift bees. Behind us was a big field of ripening corn, with a lot of poppies like blood-spatters in it, bright crimson in the rusty gold. The old man sat well forward, his vein-knotted arms laid flat along his trousers which were pulled up tight, showing his carefully polished boots.

I can't remember much of what the old man said. Mostly he talked about his mole-trapping days, or about his own boyhood, when he'd lived down South. He still had a trace of the Southern way of talking and it was perhaps that that gave his voice such a tickly, sleepy sound. But somehow the mole-trapping was not true to the old man's character as I saw it. A lot of things I said or did would bring a momentary clot of sadness into his hazel eyes.

Once I talked the old man into taking me out fishing. I made him give a solemn promise to catch me a trout. I couldn't catch a trout myself, hard as I tried, every day. Still, the fish there were lovely to look at – fat and sleek, though a bit on the fly side, I thought.

When the old man had said he would take me fishing, we went round to the back of the cottage to gather worms from the hen-coop. The coop was round in the long, narrow garden the old man looked after, with the help of his sister, who was tying string round the currant bushes just then, as we began to dig the worms. The old man suffered from rheumatism, so he held the worm-tin while I dug at the dunged soil with a fork.

It must have been a very hot day, for I remember the old man had first unbuttoned his waistcoat, then taken it off and hung it on a bush. His woolly vest showed white through the slits in his thick, grey shirt. Once I broke a worm in half as I was pulling it from its escape-hole, and he stepped forward and ground the bits to nothing with his polished boot. 'They have feelings the same as we do,' he said, looking at me gently. As he spoke, the apple in his throat wobbled up and down, and I was suddenly saddened to see the brown crinkles in his neck, where his shirt-collar was missing. Then his sister called over to him from among the currant-bushes, and while he was gone to help her knot the string, I gathered up the worms and we were ready to start.

I took my rod from the shed where I always left it, never taking the pieces down, or untying the hook. It was an old shed. In the dusty corners of it stood cobwebbed washing-mangles, and the kind of big, brass basins in which black-currant jam is made in season. There was a steady drip of sunlight through the tiles down to the floor of brown earth. I liked just to stand in there, sniffing the dusty-damp smell which reminded me of some-thing – something I could almost, but never quite remember.

The blue tar on the road had melted in the heat, and I left the marks of my rubber-heeled shoes on it as I walked along. At first, the old man carried the fishing rod while I was left to carry the tin of worms. It was an old treacle tin with a tight-fitting lid in which I had made a few holes with a hammer and nail. 'They have to breathe the same as we do,' I thought of the old man saying. I carried the tin inside my shirt to keep the worms cool and wet. I was scared they might close up like accordions and become no good for the trout.

It was almost no distance from the cottage down to the stream. On the way, though, we had to go by the Big House. Just as we drew level with the lawn, with its neat rhododendron bushes, the old man put the fishing rod into my free hand, and looked away into the fields on the other side of the road, as if he had caught sight of something. I could not see anything there myself. He took back the rod as soon as we were by the Big House and in sight of the stream.

Now that I could see the water running out from the bridge, I thought it might be better after all if it was me who fished. But I waited behind the old man while he slowly climbed the fence. Then we began to make our way down the bank of the stream which was grown all over with a strange kind of weed, like garden rhubarb that had jumped a wall and gone wild. This weed, said the old man, would hide us from the trout.

Instead of starting to fish right away, as I knew we ought to, we walked on down to the deep corner pool. There, the old man stopped, and soon we sat down among the false rhubarb. Flies buzzed round us noisily. A motor-bicycle whizzed up the road, leaving its sound spread out behind it like a long, black snake.

The pool was dappled on the far side with the shadows of trees. The clear water, as it swirled among their roots, was soiled by a drain that poured out rusty stuff, the colour of spate. It certainly was a fine place to fish the worm. I knew that several big trout lived under the trees, for I had often seen them feeding there, from the other bank. They always ignored the worms I threw down to them, except when I threw just the worms without the hook.

At length, the old man screwed himself up to spear on a worm. He told me to sit still where I was, and not to stand up, or shout, or I would scare the fish. Then he began to crawl towards the pool carrying the rod in one hand, and, with the other, clearing away the stems of the weed. The big green leaves kept closing back like the sea. I had to stand up just a little to see him cast. He threw the worm out in a way I thought terribly clumsy. It fell just by luck, though, in the mouth of the drain and began to float down slowly into the shadow of the trees.

To my surprise, the old man laid down the rod with its tip balanced on the edge of a rhubarb leaf. He crawled back towards me, and I could feel him creak. Seeing that I had half-stood up, he waved his hand at me, and I dropped down so as not to spoil his crazy fishing. At the same time I kept my eye on the tip of the rod. Almost at once, it was jerked down from the leaf. A trout had taken the worm. I shouted, and the old man stood up and made a grab for the butt.

Except once in a fishmonger's shop, I had never been so near to a big trout. While the old man wound hurriedly at the handle of the reel, the trout followed upstream in a slow, aloof sort of way. At first, I thought he was going to snag the gut on the barbed-wire cattle-fence which ran across the shallow water at the top of the pool. But he suddenly turned and swam back down towards the roots of the trees. He could not quite reach them because of the dragging line. He leaped out from the water with a big splash then surprised us both by swimming almost to our feet. I could see the red spots on his sides, and his baleful eyes. Then he swam away again, taking the slack of the line.

While the trout splashed in the water, in the shadow of the trees, the old man looked around for a place to land him but there was simply nowhere. The banks were steep, and we had no landing-net. It was a rotten situation.

At length the fish began to turn sideways on the top of the water, and the old man reeled him across the pool till he lay right below us. He lay almost on his back, with his mouth opening slowly and regularly as a clock ticks at night. All at once I felt sorry for him and I wished we had him on the bank.

The old man handed me the rod, and began to push up his jacket sleeve to above his elbow. Then he kneeled down over the trout, and closed his fingers on it, below the gills. He was raising it from the water when suddenly it slipped, and he was left holding only the gut, broken off a good way above the hook. I dropped the rod and looked after the fish as it swam away, with my hook in it.

The old man stood quite still for several minutes, looking after the trout. Then I picked up the rod and the worm-tin, and we walked up the road to the house, saying not a word to each other. I was worried about losing the hook but, as it happened, I had another one hidden away among the hankies in my drawer. I stopped worrying. I went in for my tea, and while I was eating I saw the old man's stooped figure cross the window, and I heard his chair scrape back as – it must have been – he took off his boots.

When I had finished my tea, I went out and sat on the bench sort of waiting for the old man. He didn't come, so in the end I went along and knocked on his door. It was his sister who answered my knock. She was wiping her red hands on a white dish-cloth, while behind her I could see the wallpaper with its pattern of faded roses, and a wooden coat-stand with a pair of the old man's galoshes down below. She took me through to the kitchen where the old man was sitting in a chair drawn in by the fire.

When he saw me come in he sat up. A grey shawl was thrown about his shoulders. He had taken his stocking-soles to ease his feet, and his boots were laid by in the hearth, the firelight dancing in the polished leather. His sister told me he got the rheumatism from being down at the stream fishing, but the old man said it was a sure sign of rain. That cheered me up.

I did not wait long in the old man's private kitchen. He was going to bathe his feet in a papier-mâché basin which his sister carried through from the scullery, and put down for him on the woolly rug. I waited only till she had filled the basin. I heard him groan as he bent forward to drag off his socks; and afterwards, when I was in the garden, I heard the water gurgling away mysteriously down the hidden drain.

Sure enough, there was rain as the old man's rheumatism prophesied. The big drops splashed on the honeysuckle bushes, outside the window, all night. I woke up early. After breakfast, though, it was still raining and I wasn't allowed to go out. Then in the afternoon it faired up, and I was let take my rod from the shed, with its new, puddled floor. The smell in there was a whole lot different that day – sad and exciting somehow. I didn't have to waste time digging for worms. They had come up to the top of the ground, and one or two of the pink ones had wriggled across the road and were squashed thinly on the blue tar. All I had to do was to lift them up.

The sunlit water looked like lentil soup. Twigs and other things were bobbing round in black ripples, and I let my worm drop in beside them and I caught a good trout. I ran back across the fields and gave it in to the old man. His sister was pleased. She put the fish on a white platter, with little bits of green grass still sticking to its red-spotted sides. I went in to stare at it several times before it was gutted and fried.

The next day the water was almost clear again and I couldn't get any bites. I went down, after a while, to the corner pool, to see if I could spot the big trout. I saw one big fish, but I didn't think it was him, so I went on down to the next pool, and the next one again. This pool was like a big deep hole, with a lot of rotten branches half-buried in the mud down at the bottom of it. It was a pool where you could easily lose all your hooks.

I was just going to walk right by the pool, as I usually did, when my eye caught on something that was glinting down on the mud. I clambered down the bank and I picked up a dead branch which snapped. I threw it away. When I had found a branch strong enough, I thrust it down through the water, and poked at the big fish to get him where I could lift him out. Little pieces of mud flaked off the bottom and whirled round him like smoke. He sank up and down like a balloon each time I thrust. When at last I was able to get hold of him, I dropped him on the bank and he was quite stiff. A blue-bottle came and crawled on his eye but I shooed it away.

After I had looked at him for a long time, I took out my pen-knife and got back my hook. It was a little rusted, of course, but there was enough of the bloodied gut left to tie back on my line. I wondered what I ought to do with the trout and, eventually, I pushed him into a hole in the bank and pulled the long grass down on top.

When I had done fishing and got back to the house, the old man was sitting out on the garden bench waiting for me. His rheumatism was a bit better, and he yarned for a while about moles, and said it was an awful pity we'd lost the big trout. It was on the tip of my tongue to tell him what had happened, but I never did for I guessed that if I had it would have broken his heart.

# Clay

LEWIS GRASSIC GIBBON 1934

Across the world, more and more people move away from the country-side to live in the towns. But the land continues to attract, to inspire, and even to enslave some people. 'Clay' is one of the classic shorter fictions of Lewis Grassic Gibbon (1901–35), and shows what happens when a man loves the land so much that his passion becomes an obsession. The obsession becomes folly – or heroism?

The setting is Kincardineshire and the Howe of the Mearns, still prime farming country.

The Galts were so thick on the land around Segget folk said if you went for a walk at night and you trod on some thing and it gave a squiggle, it was ten to one you would find it a Galt. And if you were a newcomer up in the Howe and you stopped a man and asked him the way the chances were he'd be one of the brood. Like as not, before he had finished with you, he'd have sold you a horse or else stolen your watch, found out everything that you ever had done, recognised your mother and had doubts of your father. Syne off home he'd go and spread the news round from Galt of Catcraig that lay high in the hills to Galt of Drumbogs that lay low by Mondynes, all your doings were known and what you had said, what you wore next your skin, what you had to your breakfast, what you whispered to your wife in the dead of night. And the Galts would snigger *Ay, gentry, no doubt*, and spit in the vulgar way that they had: the average Galt knew less of politeness than a broody hen knows of Bible exegesis.

They farmed here and they farmed there, brothers and cousins and half-brothers and uncles, your head would reel as you tried to make out if Sarah were daughter to Ake of Catcraig or only a relation through marrying a nephew of Sim of High Rigs that was cousin to Will. But the Galts knew all their relationships fine, more especially if anything had gone a bit wrong, they'd tell you how twenty-five years or so back when the daughter of Redleaf had married her cousin, old Alec that now was the farmer of Kirn, the first bit bairn that came of that marriage – ay, faith, that bairn had come unco soon! And they'd lick at their chops as they minded of that and sneer

Farmers washing cattle, Royal Highland Show, Ingliston, near Edinburgh

at each other and fair have a time. But if you were strange and would chance to agree, they'd close up quick, with a look on their faces as much as to say *And who are you would say ill of the Galts?*

They made silver like dirt wherever they sat, there was hardly a toun that they sat in for long. So soon's they moved in to some fresh bit farm they'd rive up the earth, manure it with fish, work the land to death in the space of their lease, syne flit to the other side of the Howe with the land left dry as a rat-sucked swede. And often enough as he neared his lease-end a Galt would break and be rouped from his place, he'd say that farming was just infernal and his wife would weep as she watched her bit things sold here and there to cover their debts. And if you didn't know much of the Galts you would be right sorry and would bid fell high. Syne you'd hear in less than a six month's time that the childe that went broke had bought a new farm and had stocked it up to the hilt with the silver he'd laid cannily by before he went broke.

Well, the best of the bunch was Rob Galt of Drumbogs, lightsome and hearty, not mean like the rest, he'd worked for nearly a twenty-five years as his father's foreman up at Drumbogs. Old Galt, the father, seemed nearly immortal, the older he grew the coarser he was, Rob stuck the brute as a good son should though aye he had wanted land of his own. When they fell out at last Rob Galt gave a laugh *You can keep Drumbogs and all things that are on it, I'll soon get a place of my own, old man.* His father sneered *You?* and Rob Galt said *Ay, a place of my own and parks that are MINE.*

He was lanky and long like all of the Galts, his mouser twisted up at the ends, with a chinny Galt face and a long, thin nose, and eyes pale-blue in a red-weathered face, a fine, frank childe that was kindness itself, though his notion of taking a rest from the plough was to loosen his horses and start in to harrow. He didn't look long for a toun of his own, Pittaulds by Segget he leased in a wink, it stood high up on the edge of the Mounth, you could see the clutter of Segget below, wet, with the glint of its roofs at dawn. The rent was low, for the land was coarse, red clay that sucked with a hungry mouth at your feet as you passed through the evening fields.

Well, he moved to Pittaulds in the autumn term, folk watched his flitting come down by Mondynes and turn at the corner and trudge up the brae to the big house poised on the edge of the hill. He brought his wife, she was long as himself, with a dark-like face, quiet, as though gentry – faith, that was funny, a Gald wedded decent! But he fair was fond of the creature, folk said, queer in a man with a wife that had managed to bring but one bairn into the world. That bairn was now near a twelve years old, dark, like her mother, solemn and slim, Rob spoiled them both, the wife and the quean, you'd have thought them sugar he was feared would melt.

But they'd hardly sat down a week in Pittaulds when Rachel that would trot at the rear of Rob, like a collie dog, saw a queer-like change. Now and then her father would give her a pat and she'd think that he was to play as of old. But instead he would cry *Losh, run to the house, and see if your mother will let you come out, we've two loads of turnips to pull afore dinner.* Rachel, the quean, would chirp *Ay, father,* and go blithe to the shed for her tailer and his, and out they would wade through the cling of the clay and pull side by side down the long, swede rows, the rain in a drifting seep from the hills, below them the Howe in its garment of mist. And the little, dark quean would work by his side, say never a word though she fair was soaked; and at last go home; and her mother would stare, whatever in the world had happened to Rob? She would ask him that as he came into dinner – *the quean'll fair have her death of cold.* He would blink with his pale-blue eyes, impatient, *Hoots, lassie, she'll take no harm from the rain. And we fair must clear the swedes from the land, I'm a good three weeks behind with the work.*

The best of the Galts? Then God keep off the rest! For, as that year wore on to its winter, while he'd rise at five, as most other folk did, he wouldn't be into his bed till near morning, it was chave, chave, chave till at last you would think he'd turn himself into an earthworm, near. In the blink of the light from the lanterns of dawn he would snap short-tempered at his dark-faced wife, she would stare and wonder and give a bit laugh, and eat up his porridge as though he was feared he would lose his appetite halfway through, and muck out the byre and the stable as fast as though he were paid for the job by the hour, with a scowl of ill-nature behind his long nose. And then, while the dark still lay on the land, and through the low mist that slept on the fields not a bird was cheeping and not a thing showing but the waving lanterns in the Segget wynds, he'd harness his horses and lead out the first, its hooves striking fire from the stones of the close, and cry to the second, and it would come after, and the two of them drink at the trough while Rob would button up his collar against the sharp drive of the frozen dew as the north wind woke. Then he'd jump on the back of the meikle roan, Jim, and go swaying and jangling down by the hedge, in the dark, the

world on the morning's edge, wet, the smell of the parks in his face, the
squelch of the horses soft in the clay.

Syne, as the light came grey in a tide, wan and slow from the Bervie
Braes, and a hare would scuttle away through the grass and the peesies
waken and cry and wheep, Rob Galt would jump from the back of Jim and
back the pair up against the plough and unloose the chains from the horses'
britchins and hook them up to the swiveltrees. Then he'd spit on his hands
and cry *Wissh, Jim!* no longer ill-natured, but high-out and pleased, and
swink the plough into the red, soaked land; and the horses would strain and
snort and move canny and the clay wheel back in the coulter's trace, Rob
swaying slow in the rear of the plough, one foot in the drill and one on the
rig. The bothy billies on Arbuthnott's bents riding their pairs to start on
some park would cry one to the other *Ay, Rob's on the go,* seeing him then
as the light grew strong, wheeling, him and his horses and plough, a ranging
of dots on the park that sloped its long clay rigs to the edge of the moor.

By eight, as Rachel set out for school, a slim, dark thing with her
well-tacked boots, she would hear the whistle of her father, Rob, deep, a
wheeber upon the hill; and she'd see him coming swinging to the end of a
rig and mind how he once would stop and would joke and tease her for lads
that she had at the school. And she'd cry *Hello father!* but Rob would say
nothing till he'd drawn his horse out and looked back at the rig and given
his mouser a twist and a wipe. Syne he'd peck at his daughter as though he'd
new woke *Ay, then, so you're off,* and cry *Wissh!* to his horses and turn
them about and set to again, while Rachel went on, quiet, with the wonder
clouding her face that had altered so since she came to Pittaulds.

He'd the place all ploughed ere December was out, folk said that he'd
follow the usual Galt course, he'd showed up mean as the rest of them did,
he'd be off to the marts and a dealing in horses, or a buying of this or a
stealing of that, if there were silver in the selling of frogs the Galts would
puddock-hunt in their parks. But instead he began on the daftest-like ploy,
between the hill of Pittaulds and the house a stretch of the moor thrust in a
thin tongue, three or four acre, deep-pitted with holes and as rank with
whins as a haddock with scales, not a tenant yet who had farmed Pittaulds
but had had the sense to leave it a-be. But Rob Galt set in to break up the
land, he said it fair cried to have a man at it, he carted great stones to fill up
the holes and would lever out the roots when he could with a pick, when he
couldn't he'd bring out his horses and yoke them and tear them out from the

A Highland shepherd and his dog, about 1930

ground that way. Working that Spring to break in the moor by April's end he was all behind, folk took a laugh, it served the fool fine.

Once in a blue moon or so he'd come round, he fair was a deave as he sat by your fire, he and your man would start in on the crops and the lie of the land and how you should drain it, the best kind of turnips to plant in the clay, the manure that would bring the best yield a dry year. Your man would be keen enough on all that, but not like Rob Galt, he would kittle up daft and start in to tell you tales of the land that were just plain stite, of this park and that as though they were women you'd to prig and to pat afore they'd come on. And your man would go ganting wide as a gate and the clock would be hirpling the hours on to morn and still Rob Galt would sit here and habber. *Man, she's fairly a bitch, is that park, sly and sleeked, you can feel it as soon as you start in on her, she'll take corn with the meikle husk, not with the little. But I'll kittle her up with some phosphate, I think.* Your man would say *Ay, well, well, is that so? What do you think of this business of Tariffs?* and Rob would say *Well, man, I just couldn't say. What worries me's the park where I've put in the tares. It's fair on the sulk about something or other.*

And what could you think of a fool like that? Though he'd fallen behind with his chave on the moor he soon made it up with his working at night, he fair had a fine bit crop the next year, the wife and the quean both out at the cutting, binding and stooking as he reapered the fields. Rachel had shot up all of a sudden, you looked at her in a kind of surprise as you saw the creature go by to the school. It was said that she fair was a scholar, the quean – no better than your own bit Johnnie, you knew, the teachers were coarse to your Johnnie, the tinks. Well, Rachel brought home to Pittaulds some news the night that Rob came back from the mart, he'd sold his corn at a fair bit price. For once he had finished pleitering outside, he sat in the kitchen, his feet to the fire, puffing at his pipe, his eye on the window watching the ley rise up outside and peer in the house as though looking for him. It was Rachel thought that as she sat at her supper, dark, quiet, a bit queer, over thin to be bonny, you like a lass with a good bit of beef. Well, she finished her meat and syne started to tell the message that Dominie had sent her home with; and maybe if she was sent to the college she'd win a bursary or something to help.

Her mother said *Well, Rob, what say you to that?* and Rob asked *What?*

and they told him again and Rob skeughed his face round *What, money for school? And where do you think that I'll manage to get that?*

Mrs Galt said *Out of the corn you've just sold*, and Rob gave a laugh as though speaking to a daftie – *I've my seed to get and my drains to dig and what about the ley for the next year's corn? Damn't, it's just crying aloud for manure, it'll hardly leave me a penny-piece over.*

Rachel sat still and looked out at the ley, sitting so still, with her face in the dark. Then they heard her sniff and Rob swung round fair astonished at the sound she made. *What ails you?* he asked, and her mother said *Ails her? You would greet yourself if you saw your life ruined.* Rob got to his feet and gave Rachel a pat. *Well, well, I'm right sorry that you're taking't like that. But losh, it's a small bit thing to greet over. Come out and we'll go for a walk round the parks.*

So Rachel went with him half-hoping he thought to change his mind on this business of college. But all that he did on the walk was to stand now and then and stare at the flow of the stubble or laugh queer-like as they came to a patch where the grass was bare and the crop had failed. *Ay, see that, Rachel, the wretch wouldn't take. She'll want a deep drill, this park, the next season.* And he bent down and picked up a handful of earth and trickled the stuff through his fingers, slow, then dusted it back on the park, not the path, careful, as though it were gold-dust not dirt. So they came at last to the moor he had broken, he smoked his pipe and he stood and looked at it *Ay, quean, I've got you in fettle at last.* He was speaking to the park not his daughter but Rachel hated Pittaulds from that moment, she thought, quiet, watching her father and thinking how much he'd changed since he first set foot on its clay.

He worked from dawn until dark, and still later, he hove great harvests out of the land, he was mean as dirt with the silver he made; but in five years' time of his farming there he'd but hardly a penny he could call his own. Every merk that he got from the crops of one year seemed to cry to go back to the crops of the next. The coarse bit moor that lay north of the biggings he coddled as though 'twas his own blood and bone, he fed it manure and cross-ploughed it twice-thrice, and would harrow it, tend it, and roll the damn thing till the Segget joke seemed more than a joke, that he'd take it to bed with him if he could. For all that his wife saw of him in hers he might well have done that, Mrs Galt that was tall and dark and so quiet came to look at him queer as he came in by, you could hardly believe it still was the Rob that once wouldn't blush to call you his jewel, that had many a time said all he wanted on earth was a wife like he had and land of his own. But that was afore he had gotten the land.

One night she said as they sat at their meat *Rob, I've still that queer pain in my breast. I've had it for long and I doubt that it's worse. We'll need to send for the doctor, I think.* Rob said *Eh?* and gleyed at her dull *Well, well, that's fine. I'll need to be stepping, I must put in a two-three hours the night on the weeds that are coming so thick in the swedes, it's fair pestered with the dirt, that poor bit of park.* Mrs Galt said *Rob, will you leave your parks, just for a minute, and consider me? I'm ill and I want a doctor at last.*

Late the next afternoon he set off for Stonehive and the light came low and the hours went by, Mrs Galt saw nothing of her man or the doctor and near went daft with the worry and pain. But at last as it grew fell black on the fields she heard the step of Rob on the close and she ran out and cried *What's kept you so long?* and he said *What's that? Why, what but my work?* He'd come back and he'd seen his swedes waiting the hoe, so he'd got off his bike and held into the hoeing, what sense would there have been in wasting his time going up to the house to tell the news that the doctor wouldn't be till the morn?

Well, the doctor came in his long brown car, he cried to Rob as he hoed the swedes *I'll need you up at the house with me.* And Rob cried *Why? I've no time to waste.* But he got at last into the doctor's car and drove to the house and waited impatient; and the doctor came ben, and was stroking his lips; and he said *Well, Galt, I'm feared I've bad news. Your wife has a cancer of the breast, I think.*

She'd to take to her bed and was there a good month while Rob Galt worked the Pittaulds on his own. Syne she wrote a letter to her daughter Rachel that was fee'd in Segget, and Rachel came home. And she said, quiet, *Mother, has he never looked near you? I'll get the police on the beast for this,* she meant her own father that was out with the hay, through the windows she could see him scything a bout, hear the skirl of the stone as he'd whet the wet blade, the sun a still lowe on the drowsing Howe, the dying woman in the littered bed. But Mrs Galt whispered *He just doesn't think, it's not that he's cruel, he's just mad on Pittaulds.*

But Rachel was nearly a woman by then, dark, with a temper that all the lads knew, and she hardly waited for her father to come home to tell him how much he might well be ashamed, he had nearly killed her mother with neglect, was he just a beast with no heart at all? But Rob hardly looked at the quean in his hurry *Hoots, lassie, your stomach's gone sour with the heat. Could I leave my parks to get covered with weeds?* And he gave her a pat, as to quieten a bairn, and ate up his dinner, all in a fash to be coling the hay. Rachel cried *Aren't you going to look in on mother?* and he said *Oh, ay,* and went ben in a hurry. *Well, lass, you'll be pleased that the hay's done fine – Damn't, there's a cloud coming up from the sea!* And the next that they saw he was out of the house staring at the cloud as at Judgment Day.

Mrs Galt was dead ere September's end, on the day of the funeral as folk came up they met Rob Galt in his old cord breeks, with a hoe in his hand, and he said he'd been out loosening up the potato drills a wee bit. He changed to his black and he helped with his brothers to carry the coffin out to the hearse. There were three bit carriages, he got in the first, and the horses went jangling slow to the road. The folk in the carriage kept solemn and long-faced, they thought Rob the same because of his wife. But he suddenly woke *Damn't, man, but I've got it! It's LIME that I should have given the yavil. It's been greeting for the stuff, that park on the brae!*

Rachel took on the housekeeping at Pittaulds, sombre and slim, aye reading in books, she would stand of a winter night and listen to the suck and slob of the rain on the clay, and hate the sound as she tried to hate Rob. And sometimes he'd say as they sat at their meat *What's wrong with you, lass, that you're glowering like that?* and the quean would look down, and remember her mother, while Rob rose cheery and went to his work.

And yet, as she told to one of the lads that came cycling up from Segget to see her, she just couldn't hate him, hard though she tried. There was something in him that tugged at herself daft-like, a feeling with him that the fields mattered and mattered, nothing else at all. And the lad said *What, not even me, Rachel?* and she laughed and gave him that which he sought, but half-absent like, she thought little of lads.

Well, that winter Rob Galt made up his mind that he'd break in another bit stretch of the moor beyond the bit he already had broke, there the land rose steep in a birn of wee braes, folk told him he fair would be daft to break that, it was land had lain wild and unfed since the Flood. Rob Galt said *Maybe, but they're queer-like, those braes, as though some childe had once shored them tight up.* And he set to the trauchle as he'd done before, he'd come sweating in like a bull at night and Rachel would ask him *Why don't you rest?* and he'd stare at her dumbfounded a moment: *What, rest, and me with my new bit park? What would I do but get on with my work?*

And then, as the next day wore to its close, she heard him crying her name outbye, and went through the close, and he waved from the moor. So she closed the door and went up by the track through the schlorich of the wet November moor, a windy day in the winter's nieve, the hills a-cower from the bite of the wind, the whins in that wind had a moan as they moved, not a day for a dog to be out you would say. But she found her father near tirred to the skin, he'd been heaving a great root up from its hold, *Come in by and look on this fairly, lass, I knew that some childe had once farmed up here.*

And Rachel looked at the hole in the clay and the chamber behind it, dim in the light, where there gleamed a rickle of stone-grey sticks, the bones of a man of antique time. Amid the bones was a litter of flints and a crumbling stick in the shape of a heuch.

She knew it as an eirde of olden time, an earth-house built by the early folk. Rob nodded, *Ay, he was more than that. Look at that heuch, it once scythed Pittaulds. Losh, lass, I'd have liked to have kenned that childe, what a crack together we'd have had on the crops!*

Well, that night Rob started to splutter and hoast, next morning was over stiff to move, fair clean amazed at his own condition. Rachel got a neighbour to go for the doctor, Rob had taken a cold while he stood and looked at the hole and the bones in the old-time grave. There was nothing in that and it fair was a shock when folk heard the news in a two-three days Rob Galt was dead of the cold he had ta'en. He'd worked all his go in the ground and nought left to fight the black hoast that took hold of his lungs.

He'd said hardly a word, once whispered *The Ley!* the last hour as he lay and looked out at that park, red-white, with a tremor of its earthen face as the evening glow came over the Howe. Then he said to Rachel *You'll take on the land, you and some childe, I've a notion for that?* But she couldn't lie even to please him just then, she'd no fancy for either the land or a lad, she shook her head and Rob's gley grew dim.

When the doctor came in he found Rob dead, with his face to the wall and the blinds down-drawn. He asked the quean if she'd stay there alone, all the night with her father's corpse? She nodded *Oh, yes,* and watched him go, standing at the door as he drove off to Segget. Then she turned her about and went up through the parks, quiet, in the wet, quiet gloaming's coming, up through the hill to the old earth-house.

There the wind came sudden in a gust in her hair as she looked at the place and the way she had come and thought of the things the minister would say when she told him she planned her father be buried up here by the bones of the man of old time. And she shivered sudden as she looked round about at the bare clay slopes that slept in the dusk, the whistle of the whins seemed to rise in a voice, the parks below to whisper and listen as the wind came up them out of the east.

All life – just clay that awoke and strove to return again to its mother's breast. And she thought of the men who had made these rigs and the windy days of their toil and years, the daftness of toil that had been Rob Galt's, that had been that of many men long on the land, though seldom seen now, was it good, was it bad? What power had that been that woke once on this brae and was gone at last from the parks of Pittaulds?

For she knew in that moment that no other would come to tend the ill rigs in the north wind's blow. This was finished and ended, a thing put by, and the whins and the broom creep down once again, and only the peesies wheep and be still when she'd gone to the life that was hers, that was different, and the earth turn sleeping, unquieted no longer, her hungry bairns in her hungry breast where sleep and death and the earth were one.

# The Kitten

ALEXANDER REID 1950s

This is a farming story, from the same rural world as 'Clay' (page 27) and 'Touch and Go!' (page 44). It reminds us that the land doesn't just belong to humans, but has other wild inhabitants. Find out what happens when a farm worker has to get rid of a few kittens. Sometimes, the gentle and the harmless may not be quite what they seem to be . . .

The feet were tramping directly towards her. In the hot darkness under the tarpaulin the cat cuffed a kitten to silence and listened intently.

She could hear the scruffling and scratching of hens about the straw-littered yard; the muffled grumbling of the turning churn in the dairy; the faint clink and jangle of harness from the stable – drowsy, comfortable, reassuring noises through which the clang of the iron-shod boots on the cobbles broke ominously.

The boots ground to a halt, and three holes in the cover, brilliant, diamond-points of light, went suddenly black. Crouching, the cat waited, then sneezed and drew back as the tarpaulin was thrown up and glaring white sunlight struck at her eyes.

She stood over her kittens, the fur of her back bristling and the pupils of her eyes narrowed to pin-points. A kitten mewed plaintively.

For a moment, the hired man stared stupidly at his discovery, then turned towards the stable and called harshly: 'Hi, Maister! Here a wee.'

A second pair of boots clattered across the yard, and the face of the farmer, elderly, dark and taciturn, turned down on the cats.

'So that's whaur she's been,' commented the newcomer slowly.

He bent down to count the kittens and the cat struck at him, scoring a red furrow across the back of his wrist. He caught her by the neck and flung her roughly aside. Mewing she came back and began to lick her kittens. The Master turned away.

'Get rid of them,' he ordered. 'There's ower mony cats aboot this place.'

'Aye, Maister,' said the hired man.

Catching the mother he carried her, struggling and swearing, to the stable, flung her in, and latched the door. From the loft he secured an old potato sack and with this in his hand returned to the kittens.

There were five, and he noticed their tigerish markings without comprehending as, one by one, he caught them and thrust them into the bag. They were old enough to struggle, spitting, clawing and biting at his fingers.

Throwing the bag over his shoulder he stumped down the hill to the burn, stopping twice on the way to wipe the sweat that trickled down his face and neck, rising in beads between the roots of his lint-white hair.

Behind him, the buildings of the farm-steading shimmered in the heat. The few trees on the slope raised dry, brittle branches towards a sky bleached almost white. The smell of the farm, mingled with peat-reek, dung, cattle, milk, and the dark tang of the soil, was strong in his nostrils, and when he halted there was no sound but his own breathing and the liquid burbling of the burn.

Throwing the sack on the bank, he stepped into the stream. The water was low, and grasping a great boulder in the bed of the burn he strained to lift it, intending to make a pool.

He felt no reluctance at performing the execution. He had no feelings about the matter. He had drowned kittens before. He would drown them again.

Panting with his exertion, the hired man cupped water between his hands and dashed it over his face and neck in a glistening shower. Then he turned to the sack and its prisoners.

He was in time to catch the second kitten as it struggled out of the bag. Thrusting it back and twisting the mouth of the sack close, he went after the other. Hurrying on the sun-browned grass, treacherous as ice, he slipped and fell headlong, but grasped the runaway in his outflung hand.

It writhed round immediately and sank needle-sharp teeth into his thumb so that he grunted with pain and shook it from him. Unhurt, it fell by a clump of whins and took cover beneath them.

The hired man, his stolidity shaken by frustration, tried to follow. The whins were thick and, scratched for his pains, he drew back, swearing flatly, without colour or passion.

Stooping he could see the eyes of the kitten staring at him from the shadows under the whins. Its back was arched, its fur erect, its mouth open, and its thin lips drawn back over its tiny white teeth.

The hired man saw, again without understanding, the beginnings of tufts on the flattened ears. In his dull mind he felt a dark resentment at this creature which defied him. Rising, he passed his hand up his face in heavy thought, then slithering down to the stream, he began to gather stones. With an armful of small water-washed pebbles he returned to the whins.

First he strove to strike at the kitten from above. The roof of the whins was matted and resilient. The stones could not penetrate it. He flung straight then – to maim or kill – but the angle was difficult and only one missile reached its mark, rebounding from the ground and striking the kitten a glancing blow on the shoulder.

Kneeling, his last stone gone, the hired man watched, the red in his face deepening and thin threads of crimson rising in the whites of his eyes as the blood mounted to his head. A red glow of anger was spreading through his brain. His mouth worked and twisted to an ugly rent.

'Wait – wait,' he cried hoarsely, and, turning, ran heavily up the slope to the trees. He swung his whole weight on a low-hanging branch, snapping it off with a crack like a gun-shot.

Seated on the warm, short turf, the hired man prepared his weapon, paring at the end of the branch till the point was sharp as a dagger. When it was ready he knelt on his left knee and swung the branch to find the balance. The kitten was almost caught.

The savage lance-thrust would have skewered its body as a trout is spiked on the beak of a heron, but the point, slung too low, caught in a fibrous root and snapped off short. Impotently the man jabbed with his broken weapon while the kitten retreated disdainfully to the opposite fringe of the whins.

In the slow-moving mind of the hired man the need to destroy the kitten had become an obsession. Intent on this victim, he forgot the others abandoned by the burn side; forgot the passage of time, and the hard labour of the day behind him. The kitten, in his distorted mind, had grown to a monstrous thing, centring all the frustrations of a brutish existence. He craved to kill . . .

But so far the honours lay with the antagonist.

In a sudden flash of fury the man made a second bodily assault on the whins and a second time retired defeated.

He sat down on the grass to consider the next move as the first breath of the breeze wandered up the hill. As though that were the signal, in the last moments of the sun, a lark rose, close at hand, and mounted the sky on the flood of its own melody.

The man drank in the coolness thankfully, and, taking a pipe from his pocket, lit the embers of tobacco in the bowl. He flung the match from him,

Scottish wildcat: a museum specimen. The wildcat is now an endangered species in Scotland.

still alight, and a dragon's tongue of amber flame ran over the dry grass before the breeze, reached a bare patch of sand and flickered out. Watching it, the hired man knitted his brows and remembered the heather-burning, and mountain hares that ran before the scarlet terror. And he looked at the whins.

The first match blew out in the freshening wind, but at the second the bush burst into crackling flame.

The whins were alight on the leeward side and burned slowly against the wind. Smoke rose thickly, and sparks and lighted shivers of wood sailed off on the wind to light new fires on the grass of the hillside.

Coughing as the pungent smoke entered his lungs, the man circled the clump till the fire was between him and the farm. He could see the kitten giving ground slowly before the flame. He thought for a moment of lighting this side of the clump also and trapping it between two fires; took his matches from his pocket, hesitated, and replaced them. He could wait.

Slowly, very slowly, the kitten backed towards him. The wind fought for it, delaying, almost holding the advance of the fire through the whins.

Showers of sparks leaped up from the bushes that crackled and spluttered as they burned, but louder than the crackling of the whins, from the farm on the slope of the hill, came another noise – the clamour of voices. The hired man walked clear of the smoke that obscured his view and stared up the hill.

The thatch of the farmhouse, dry as tinder, was aflare.

Gaping, he saw the flames spread to the roof of the byre, to the stables; saw the farmer running the horses to safety, and heard the thunder of hooves as the scared cattle, turned loose, rushed from the yard. He saw a roof collapse in an uprush of smoke and sparks, while a kitten, whose sire was a wild cat, passed out of the whins unnoticed and took refuge in a deserted burrow.

From there, with cold, defiant eyes, it regarded the hired man steadfastly.

# Touch and Go!

DAVID TOULMIN 1972

The 1930s were a hard time for farm workers. What to do, if your husband is ailing and needs nourishment, and you are poor? In this tale, possible tragedy is turned into humour when two enterprising women decide to make sure that their families are well fed. This text is written in the Doric Scots of North-east Scotland, a lively dialect which is at its best and easiest when you read it aloud. Most of the Scots words that may look difficult to you are explained in the glossary on page 140.

It was a dark winter's night that Wee Tam's mither and Mrs Lunan, a neighbour body, planned a raid on a nearby farmer's henhouse. Mrs Lunan's man was a cripple, and they lived in an old croft house down in the howe of Glenshinty. They had three or four bairns running barefoot around the place, with hardly a stitch of clothing on their backs, but somehow they managed to scrape along on a mere pittance from the Assistance Board, and once in a while the Inspector of the Poor looked in by to see if the creatures were still alive.

'Ma man's been real poorly lately,' said Mrs Lunan, warming her hands at the fire, 'and a drappie o' chicken bree wad do him a world o' good.'

'But whaur are we gaun tae get a hen at this time o' nicht?'

'Steal ane,' said Mrs Lunan, unabashed.

'Steal ane!' cried Tam's mither, and she looked at the woman half in sympathy, half in fear, wondering what she was going to say next.

'Aye, we'll try auld Grimshaw's place; it's fine near the road and naebody wad jalouse us there. Get on yer coat wife and gie us a hand.'

'A' richt wifie, but it's a bit risky,' said Tam's mither, buttoning up her coat; 'and Tam, put on yer bonnet and come and watch the coast is clear for us, and see there's nae ferlies aboot.'

Wee Tam shut his book and shuddered. He had been reading *Robinson Crusoe*, a big book that he had got from the dominie, one of those old-fashioned editions with beautifully stencilled capitals at the beginning of each chapter, and with a short summary of the events therein related. The loon was just getting fully absorbed in this pirate and cutlass masterpiece when the women hatched their plan.

The lamp was lit and the blinds were down and Tam's father snored in the box-bed. He was an early bedder and missed much of the goings on in the hoose, but Tam felt that the old man had one eye open half the time and that he listened between the snores. But he never interfered, mither was boss. Flora, Tam's little sister, lay snugly at her father's back, curled like a buckie, a doll in her oxter, and Tam felt it was a pity he hadn't gone to bed, then perhaps the women wouldn't have bothered him.

It was inky black and bitter cold outside. A mass of stars spangled the sky, and Tam could pick out the Seven Sisters twinkling above the dark smudge of pinewood on the Berry Hill. But apart from the sough and flap of the wind the world was as silent as a graveyard.

Tam shivered in his thin jacket as he trudged on behind the women, trying to identify the adventure with what he had been reading in *Robinson Crusoe*. About a mile along the road they came to Grimshaw's place, a big croft by the roadside, which Tam passed every day going to school. There was a lean-to poultry shed at the gable of the steading, close by the road, but in full view of the kitchen door.

The women first went past the farmhouse, to make sure there were no lights in the windows, walking on the grass to quieten the sound of their footsteps, then came back to where Tam waited at the henhouse.

Tam watched and listened but nobody stirred, nothing but the faint smell of the sharn midden and the scent of stale peat smoke that came to his nostrils on the wind. Everybody was asleep at this hour so the two women crept into the henhouse. They groped for a couple of good plump birds on the roost and wrung their necks before a cackle escaped them. There was some flapping of wings and a flutter of feathers when they came out, but never a squawk from the dead birds. They put the hens in a sack, closed the henhouse door and made off, Wee Tam behind them, still walking on the grass, all as silent as doomsday.

Safely home Tam went back to Robinson Crusoe Island, thinking no more about the affair, glad to be back to the fire and the lamplight, snug in the satisfaction that he could read till his eyes closed without further interruption, for it was just past midnight.

The women set to plucking the hens in the kitchen, while the birds were still warm, which makes it easier to do, and cleaning them, getting them ready for the dinner, maybe with a plate of broth first and the hen to follow, but Mrs Lunan said she would roast hers because she wanted the 'bree' for her sick man.

Tam got a helping when he got home from school, running all the way at the thought of it, his satchel unstrapped and under his arm, to save the thump of it on his back. And it had been a rare treat, especially the stuffing and the white flesh around the breast-bone, which mither had laid aside for him, and his old man had never asked where the hen came from.

In the evening, after supper, Tam was lighting a cigarette over the lamp glass on the kitchen table, when the local bobby laid his bicycle against the unblinded window. Tam quickly snibbed the fag in the fire, just as the bobby walked in, never waiting for an answer to his knock on the door.

'Aye lad,' says the bobby, as he peeled off his leather gloves. 'I fairly caught ye that time. I suppose ye ken that sixteen is the age for smokin'.'

Tam squeezed himself into the corner behind the meal barrel, his surest refuge in times of trouble. He remembered the hen in the dresser and he felt terribly guilty and afraid. His father was seated by the fireside. The policeman turned to him and said: 'Don't ye know it's illegal for the lad tae smoke afore he's sixteen?'

Tam's father scratched his balding head, tired from his day's work in the byres. 'Oh aye,' says he, wearily, 'but the laddie gie's me a hand in the byre, and for that I dinna grudge 'im a bit blaw at a fag.'

But the bobby was indignant. 'It's not a question of whether you can afford it man, but you're breaking the law!' He turned to Tam's mither, who was placing a chair for him – 'Woman,' he said, 'do ye allow this to go on in the hoose: the rascal smokin' and him still at school?'

'Oh aye, but the man's boss in the hoose here,' she lied, thankful that the tiny wish-bone from the hen was in the oven, and not on the crook over the range as it might have been. When it became thoroughly brittle Tam would share it with his little sister: each would take a splint of it in the crook of a little finger, make a wish and pull, and whoever had the broken end when the bone snapped would lose the wish.

The constable sat down on a hard chair in the middle of the cement floor, crossed his legs and laid his 'cheese-cutter' cap on his knee. He was so near the hen now he could have smelled it. He only had to reach over to open the dresser door and there was the skeleton of it, on a plate.

He was much nearer Tam's height on the varnished chair and the loon breathed a little more freely behind the meal barrel. Nevertheless he was still a mighty giant in the shabby little kitchen, his red face polished with stern authority and his silver buttons twinkling in the lamplight. Tam focused his attention on the bobby's putteed leg, which he kept swinging up and down over his knee, as if he wished to show off the highly polished boot at the end of it, a boot that would give you a hefty kick in the buttocks if he got near enough.

'Have ye seen ony strange characters in the vicinity?' the bobby asked, looking first at Tam's mither, and then at his father. 'Auld Sandy Grimshaw has missed some hens out of his shed, and says that by the mess of feathers ootside the door, he feels sure they have been stolen.'

Tam's father suddenly recalled his splendid dinner but swallowed the thought. 'No,' he said, trying to look unconcerned, 'no, we hinna seen a crater, not a crater!'

Tam's mither poured out a glass of Dr Watson's Tonic Stout for the bobby, and one for her husband. It was the only hop beverage in the house and she excelled in the brewing of it, though she sometimes made broom wine in the summer, with a taste like whisky.

'Ye ken auld Grimshaw's place?' the bobby asked, taking the glass in his fat, beringed fingers.

'Aye,' said Tam's mither, wiping her hands on her apron, 'I ken the fairm: it's at the top o' the quarry brae, nae far frae the shop.'

'Aye, ye ken wuman, I'm nae supposed tae drink in uniform, but in this case we'll mak' an exception.'

'Ach man, that stuff will never touch ye!' And Tam's mither busied herself wiping the table of what she had spilled, for the bottles were brisk and the froth had hit the roof when she removed the corks.

Tam's wee sister came forward with her biggest doll and laid it on the bobby's knee. He bent the doll forward in his huge hand and it 'Ba-a-a-ed' pitifully, as if it had a tummy ache. He only had to ask little Flora what Dolly had for dinner and he had the case wrapped up.

But the local flat-foot was no Sherlock Holmes, and he believed only what he saw; like loons smoking while still in short breeks, or a poor farm servant chauving home against the wind without a rear-light on his bicycle.

Otherwise there wasn't a feather of evidence in sight. The wing feathers were tied in a bundle in the cubby-hole under the loft stair. Tam's mither would wash them and use them to brush her oat-cakes before she put them in the girdle over the fire. The downs were concealed in a sack; she would stuff them into a pillow after they had been fumigated. The cats had eaten all the offal on the midden. There wasn't a shred of evidence left anywhere in sight.

The bobby licked his lips and set the empty glass on the table. 'Thanks mistress,' he said, wiping his moustache, 'that was capital!'

He got up and put on his peaked cap and gloves, glowering down at wee Tam behind the meal barrel. 'Ye can coont yersel' lucky lad,' he said, 'lucky that I'm nae takin' ye tae the lock-up. Gin yer mither hadna been sic a gweed-he'rtet wuman, and yer faither sic an honest decent body, I might hae run ye in for smokin'. But if I catch ye at it again I wunna be sae lenient!'

Turning to Tam's mither in the door he said: 'By the by mistress, wha bides in that hoose in the howe, alang the Laich Road?'

'Oh,' says Tam's mither, wondering what the bobby was leading to. 'It's Mrs Lunan bides there.'

The bobby was now outside on the gravel, his brass buttons shining in the light from the open doorway, for it was now quite dark. 'Mrs Lunan,' says he, still quizzical, 'and do ye think she wad hae seen onybody suspicious, or could gie us ony information?'

Tam's mither began to tremble with excitement. 'Oh I hardly think so,' she said, trying to seem unconcerned, 'she's a bittie frae the road and disna see mony strangers.'

'Ah weel,' replied the bobby, 'but I'd better look in and see her onywye. Gweed nicht mistress!'

The policeman was scarcely astride his bicycle when Mrs Lunan burst in on Tam's folk from the darkness. They had been watching the rear-light on the bobby's bike as he sped down the brae. All had seemed lost but now they crowded round Mrs Lunan in the lighted doorway, to see what could be done.

'Run wifie,' cried Tam's mither, exasperated, 'fly hame as fast as ye can, the bobby has been here and he's just left, and he's on the road tae your hoose noo. Run wifie, for heaven's sake run!'

'Michty mee!' cried the woman, 'I meant tae borrow something, but that doesna matter noo. Michty mee! Oor hen's still on the table, or what's left o't!' And away she flew, clambering over the dyke like a schoolgirl, lost in the darkness.

It was touch and go: the bobby on his bike round by the road, the woman on her feet across the wet fields. The bobby had a few minutes' start ahead of her and she had another dyke to jump, and a deep ditch lay in her path.

Wee Tam could see the bobby's light as he moved along the Laich Road, but he could only guess how the woman fared in the darkness. The bobby had a gate to open at the end of the cart-track that led to the cottage. Tam closed the lobby door to shut in the light and waited. It wouldn't do to let the bobby know they were watching. It was touch and go . . .

It was close on midnight when Mrs Lunan went panting back to Tam's mither with the news. 'Michty mee,' she gasped, 'I got hame first but just in time. It was a near thing I can tell ye. I was like tae faint and fair oot o' breath or I reached the door. I put the hen oot o' sight in the dresser, double quick. I just had time tae get my breath back when the bobby rapped on the door. I closed the lobby door so's he couldna see my face in the licht, and he never cam' ben the hoose, so he never noticed my weet shoes and stockin's. Thank heavens he didna find us oot. We wunna hae tae try that again wifie!'

Tam's mither was relieved. 'Na faith ye,' she said, 'but hoo's yer man, Mrs Lunan?'

'He's fine,' said the woman, 'but he doesna ken a thing aboot it. He's sound asleep and he thinks I bocht the hen, me that hardly has a copper penny tae clap on anither.'

'And yer bairns, Mrs Lunan; are they asleep as weel?'

'Aye. I bedded them a' doon afore I cam' up here the first time and I hinna heard a myowt fae them since than.'

Tam's mither gave her a brimming glass of Dr Watson's Tonic Stout: 'Just to cheer you up wifie,' as she said, while the froth flew from the uncorked bottle.

Wee Tam went back to the lamp glass and relit his cigarette. His old man had gone to bed but he stopped snoring immediately and raised himself on his elbow, blinking at the light. 'Ony tae in the pot wuman?' says he, looking at his wife. 'No I dinna want the stout, nae at this time o' nicht, juist a drap tae. So that was whaur the hen cam' frae, auld Grimshaw. Weel weel, she was a tasty bird onywye!'

And then he turned on Wee Tam, now seated on a kitchen chair with *Robinson Crusoe*, the fag reek rising above the open pages. 'But ye'll hae tae watch yer smokin' ma loon, and if ye dinna come tae the byre when I want ye I'll tell the bobby ye've been at it again, ye wee rascal!'

The old blackmailer, Tam thought, but it should have taught the women a lesson.

# A Matter of Behaviour

NAOMI MITCHISON 1960s

Prejudice can happen anywhere, and at any time. In this tale, a school-teacher recalls one of her former pupils, and the apparently ordinary life the girl led – except that she was a girl who had something to hide. This is a story about an outsider in modern society – a story with a sting in its tail.

I am not one for making distinctions between one sort of person and another. And besides, there are matters of behaviour which I myself, as a teacher, have tried to establish. You see, Elsie was a Tinker – that made her different. It was no use talking about regulations. The fact was that mostly all the tinker children came to my school in winter, maybe two terms, but then they would be on the road again, all summer, everything they had learned from me forgotten. Then in August, when it came to a new start, away behind all their own age. It was hard for the tinker children, right enough, though they were healthy apart from scratches and rashes that their mothers were not bothering themselves about, and maybe they were learning another set of things on the roads the travellers took, deer and birds, a fox or maybe a pair of weasels running the road, what's called wild-life these days. But could they put it in writing? Not they, so they'd be laughed at. Not by me, but by the other children, for no child is kind by nature.

But as for wee Elsie, her mother was dead and her Dadda only wanted the boys off on the roads with him when it came to the end of April and the good weather calling at them. So Elsie stayed with an old auntie that had the use of a shed and a row of kale and two cats. She barely missed a day off school. When I saw she could read to herself I gave her a few old picture books that I was throwing out and soon enough there was a tink reading the best in the class.

More than that, she was trying to keep herself clean, which was more than the old tinker wifie did. The way it was, my children would never sit next the tinks. It was the smell off them, you understand, wood smoke and little washing, with no soap. But if you lived the way the travelling folk used to, you'd not have much chance of looking a bath in the face. Mind you, it is different today; many of them with the smart caravans, the same size and make as the tourists' or better. You'll not see a woman lugging away between two barrow handles the way I'd seen them when I first took on a single teacher school with a roll of twenty dropping to fifteen, away in the west. No, it was different altogether in those days.

But Elsie managed to wash herself and her school clothes, though they were nothing great. But I found her bits of decent cloth she could work with in the sewing class. She learned to knit and I unravelled an old jersey of my own, a New Year's present, but too bright altogether for me. But for all that Elsie was slow at her writing. She persevered, yes that she did, and she picked up arithmetic, so long as it was about real things, and indeed that's how I feel about it myself. Once she was in Standard Two she made friends with a few her own age, two from the Forestry houses and one, Linda that was, from the Post Office. Respectable families and they'd ask her for tea, or rather their mothers did, maybe three or four times in the year, and pleasing themselves to feel they'd been good. But all the same they never let it drift out of their minds that wee Elsie was just a tinker.

She grew up to be a handsome figure of a girl, so she did, with that bright hair that most of the travellers have, and bright blue eyes to match it. I'd seen less of her once she went on to the Grammar School at Oban, and left on the stroke of fifteen, for the old woman was getting less able to do even the bit of cleaning she used to do and when her father and the boys were around it was Elsie who had to wash and mend their clothes and see to their dirty heads and all that. So it was hard on her. She would come over to me an odd evening and I could see she'd been crying.

Well, the years went by and, as you know, I married and we moved around, first to Dumbarton, then to Glasgow itself. But I'd enough friends around the village that would be pleased to see us both, and my own wee Ian when he came. So I kept up with the old families I'd known and I saw Elsie turn into a fine young woman, even if she had no time for anything beyond what she had to do, and then suddenly she was married.

This would have been in the early sixties, with things brightening up and all of us sure the bad times were past. There were only a few at the wedding and the old wifie was safe in the kirk-yard, but Elsie's father had smartened himself up with a red rose in his coat and so had the one brother who was still about. I liked the look of the bridegroom. His mother and sister were there and doubtless wondering what like of a lass was coming into the family. Truly, I was afraid the two tinks might make a scene and that would be hard on Elsie, but they were scared to say much. They were fou drunk by the evening, but the others were well away by then.

I went to the wedding myself. I thought it would have been kind of nice if one of her school mates, Linda or Jessie perhaps, had been there to see how bonny she looked, poor Elsie, but none of them came. (Linda was courting at that same time and married the next year. I was at her wedding too, but it was a bigger affair, with a two-tier cake.) It was only strangers or part strangers in the church, come just for the taste of a wedding. Elsie was wearing high-necked white and I wondered was it a bought dress. Her hair showed flaming under her veil and I didn't wonder a man would fall for her.

He seemed a very decent man, a welder from a steel works, and his folk pleased that I had come and at my present of a set of cups, the same I'd give to any one of my old pupils if I'd been to the wedding. They went back to one of those small towns that were springing up, Edinburgh way, but not for long. The year after they moved to Corby in England. She wrote to me from there. I think she was a wee bit scared to be out of Scotland and not always understanding what people said to her. I was kind of surprised to hear from her, but all the same I wrote back and the next year she wrote again, asking me if ever I was in the south could I not come over and see her.

I thought this hardly likely, but as things turned out my husband was sent south to a branch his firm was setting up in Kettering and that was only a bus ride from Corby. I remember it well, a beautiful, rich countryside, parts of it Buccleuch land, though what the Buccleuchs were doing this far south was beyond me. There were well-doing villages, pretty old cottages and gardens packed to the gate with rose bushes. But Corby itself was given over to steel, rows and crescents and long streets of workers' houses and all that was left of the old village not knowing itself in the middle of them. There was a great chimney, alight with flames from the furnaces below; you could see it for miles. They called it the Corby Candle.

There was a Scots club and pleasant enough to be among ken'd folk, even if they were from the far ends of Scotland. They would have concerts and that; time and again there'd be a hundred folk standing to sing Auld Lang Syne. But some were terrible homesick, worst the ones who had come from towns along the coasts, whether it was Peterhead or Campbeltown. They missed the sea sorely, here in the very middle of England. But the fishing had gone down and the money was away better down here. There were others from Wales or Cornwall or anywhere at all, but it was the Scots there were most of, and who made up the best part of the clubs, the Labour club as well.

So Elsie met me and took me back to her house, talking all the way. It was a modern house, in one of the crescents, two bedrooms and a smart bathroom. And almost all the furnishing bought: a lounge suite, the kind you'd see advertised, a table with a pot plant, new kitchen stuff, only she'd brought her old kettle and her griddle, for you'd not get one in England. But she had an electric iron and there were my tea cups, not a chip out of them. Everything was kept shining and a biscuit jar, I mind that, which they'd won in a Labour Party lottery. She showed it all to me, piece by piece, and told me not one bit of furnishing, not even the suite, was on the never-never, but all paid for. 'And nobody knows I'm a tinker!' she said and when I laughed and said she shouldn't be ashamed of that, she clutched my hand and said 'You'll not tell!'

So I said no, no, and laughed a bittie and then she took me out to her wee garden in front of the house, all newly planted with small rose bushes that still had their labels on. They'd a drill of potatoes and a few cabbages at the back. Her wee girl was at play-school – yes, they had that and all – but there was a baby boy in a pram out among the rose bushes, asleep, with a soft fuzz of orange. I said to her, laughing 'I see he has your colour of hair' and I can still hear her saying back 'I could wish it was black!' And her husband, just coming back from work, had dark hair. They were that friendly, both of them, and I went over there from time to time, with my Ian who was about the age of her wee girl. She talked sometimes of the days she'd been at school – she'd still got the books I'd given her – but not much about the other girls, only a mention of Miss McSporran who had been the infant teacher and well liked by all my pupils.

But then, as you know, my husband was moved back to Scotland and we settled down in Hillhead. I remember the last time I saw her she had a big stomach, but full of content and looking forward. So the years went by and I sometimes thought of Kettering and Corby and wondered how the friends we'd made were doing and sometimes we'd send cards. But mostly I was glad to be back in Scotland with my husband and my own two, both shooting up taller than myself, and Ian talking of what he'd be doing after

University. For my own part I was doing supply teaching, but I had begun to lose touch with my profession. And indeed, teaching in Glasgow is away different from teaching in a village.

And then, in the late seventies and eighties, the bad times came on us, with the yards closing down all along Clydeside and nowhere to turn, and all the anger breaking. And not us alone, but industry everywhere, what our forebears worked for and built up, coal, steel, shipping, the great companies that had seemed to be there forever. It seemed strange to me, since we had won the bitter war with Japan and tried and executed their Generals, that now they could be the ones who had all the factories, or else it was the Germans who had them, while our men who had fought, the older ones, in that war, were now thrown out with nothing but their old medals and the dole. What had gone wrong?

At first it did not hit us and our friends just so hard, though salary rises that my husband had expected just didn't come through. What we felt most was the terrible price that everything was, the way you had to pay a whole pound for something that was only worth what used to be half a crown in the old days. And then, well, everything got worse. But you'll know that. At least I had my two educated.

The works of Corby went. The steel industry was cut down so that it was hardly there; we didn't know what worse would follow. How had it happened? It seemed we couldn't make steel as cheaply as other countries, or it was not the kind that was wanted. We couldn't understand. Only we knew it was a matter of money, not of men working. And when money talks there's no place for people, for ordinary men and women, the like of Elsie and her man.

Well, it seemed that there could be small industries starting up here or there, maybe taking over premises in a small town and not doing too badly, at least for a few years. You've heard of TT and MCV? Yes, well they started up somewhere west of Bathgate, on some waste ground there was, and it seemed there were jobs going. A few of the Corby men heard of it. It was nothing like what they were used to and you wouldn't see the furnace men going, but those who'd been on the lighter side and willing to take training, they might have a chance. At least they'd be nearer home. The wages were nothing near Corby, but better than the dole. Yes, it had come to that. They cursed the Tory Government and this man MacGregor – but no Scot! – who'd been put in charge of the steel industry, but they went up to the new place for interview, remembered to say Sir, and were taken on. Elsie waited to hear. They sold most of the furniture, the best bits, the ones they'd been proud of, the lounge suite, the Hoover, the washing machine.

Well, I know the rest of the story by hearsay. He started work. For a while they were in one room, not easy to keep decent. And then they got half an old house, a bike ride away. The two older children, the girl and the boy, started at the new school; the girl was well up in Secondary by now and promising well. But the third child, another wee boy, was still at home. There was no kind of pre-school in those parts. The nearest was a bus-drive away and most likely full up, let alone she couldn't afford the bus fare. She tried to feed the children well and her man best; that's the way it is for most of us women.

Well, she went to a jumble sale. The children kept growing and had to be clothed. Some of the jumbles were away better than you'd get at the shops, anyway the shops where Elsie could go. The wee one was with her of course, he was a red-head the same as his brother, though it's not a true red but more of an orange. You'll know it, I'm sure. There's always a bit of snatching at the jumbles, and so it was this time. It was just bad luck that she met with an old school mate and they knew one another. Yes, they met across a boy's jacket and Linda – for it was her – said 'Ah, it's you – you dirty tink!' and a man behind said 'What, playing tinkers' tricks on us!' And poor Elsie ran out of the sale with nothing, just hauling the wee one, pulling him along crying, and maybe the good folk walking past would have stopped and scolded her, and when she got back in she saw that her purse was gone out of her pocket.

So she put the wee boy into the bedroom with what toys they had and half an orange, and herself went to the kitchen, turned on the gas and put her head in the oven.

That was how the two children back from school found her and had the sense for the boy to run to the corner and ring the police – and lucky the 'phone was working. The ambulance men found the two children practising the artificial respiration they'd learned at school – and they'd turned the gas off. And it all came out in the evening paper and I happened to read it. It was only a small piece and I only read as far as the name because I was waiting for my Peggy to come home before I'd put the kettle on and I wondered could it be Elsie. But the next morning there was a photo in the paper of the two children and I could see that the girl looked like her mother. I knew they'd been in trouble, that the man had lost his job in Corby, but she hadn't written to say where she was. No, she'd have been ashamed. But now the shame was worse. And now I was ashamed too, that I hadn't got round to writing and finding out how my old pupil was doing.

I rang the paper and got her address, saying I was a friend, and the very next day I made my way over. I remember once when I'd visited at Corby, my own Peggy asking me 'Is she really a tink?' and I said 'Yes, and I'm telling you who the tinkers were. It was they who made the weapons for the High Kings of Ireland that came over to the west of Scotland: all those beautiful swords and shields!' For that's one of the Tinker stories, though who's to know what's true and what's not? But I felt I had to get another picture told and believed, even if it wasn't the right one. Maybe it is and would account for a lot; in the old days, before my time, the tinkers really made and mended all kinds of metal things and were more welcome then than they've ever been since.

So off I went and found poor Elsie lying on a lumpy old sofa they had, wrapped in blankets and the big girl, allowed off from school, making tea and keeping an eye on the wee boy. I'd brought some cakes and we all took our tea together. I could tell from what the girl said that her father had been in a terrible taking, coming back from work to find his wife carried off to hospital and the two children, though they'd done well and the paper said so afterwards, all to bits and no tea made.

The next time I went over she was getting on fine and ashamed of what she had done, but she told me how that name that Linda had thrown at her had been that sore on her, she had just felt that nothing else she could ever do would be any good. Nothing would ever get the bad name off her back and it came out that the boy had been called a tink at school. Nobody at Corby had ever said anything against them, but now when they came back to Scotland – and she burst into tears, the poor thing. I could have sorted that Linda who had thrown it at her, and both of them my pupils. Sure as I'm a living soul, Linda would have seen that story in the papers, but not a cheep from her. Most like she'll have forgotten Elsie's married name, so there she'll be sitting at her ease. And me forgetting Linda's married name, I'm not able to get at her! But I'm hoping that someone calls her something worse than a tink, this side of Judgement Day.

# The Face

BRIAN McCABE 1989

All of us have fears, especially of the dark and the unknown. For the boy
in this story, the Face was a nightmare he didn't want to face. But in
the company of his father, he is obliged to confront it.

In the course of the story, we learn that the Face is the coalface of the
mine at Newtongrange, in Midlothian, just outside Edinburgh. It is now
closed. The reference to Bilston Glen is to another Midlothian pit,
recently privatised. Brian McCabe grew up in this environment, where
his own father was a miner.

He didn't want to see the face.

It was like a railway tunnel, except this tunnel sloped down the way, down
through the dripping darkness, down into the deep, dark ground. He could
see the dark shine of the rails and he could feel the ridges of the wooden
sleepers through the soles of his gymshoes. It was very dark. He was glad
his father was there with him.

It would be good to go back up to the daylight now, where the miners
were sitting round a brazier, eating their pieces and drinking hot tea from
big tins with wire handles. One of them had given him a piece and let him
drink some tea from his tin and had pointed to different birds and told him
their names, while the other miners talked about the pit and how it was
closing. One of them had said he'd be quite happy never to see the face
again.

He remembered the first time he'd heard about it: his father came in late
from the pit and walked into the kitchen very slowly and sat down still with
his coat on. Then he took off his bunnet and looked at it and put it on the
kitchen table and talked to his mother in the quiet voice not like his usual
voice. Like he couldn't say what he had to say, like when some of the words
get swallowed. Because somebody had got killed at the face, John Ireland
had got killed at the face, so he'd had to go to Rosewell to tell his wife. That
was why he was late. Then his mother took a hanky from her apron pocket
and sat down and started crying, and his father put his hands on her

shoulders and kissed her like it was Christmas except this was a different kind of kiss. Then his father looked up at him and nodded to him to tell him to go through to the other room, so he went through and watched TV and wondered how the face had killed John Ireland, the man who ran the boxing gym for boys, and how something terrible could make people need to kiss each other.

He could hear the water dripping from the roof of the tunnel and trickling down the walls and the scrape and crunch of his father's pit boots on the ground. They sounded too loud, but in the dark you had to hold on to sounds, like when you shut your eyes and pretended to be blind, hold on to them to stop yourself hearing what was behind them, where it was like the darkness was listening.

Every few steps he could see the wooden props against the walls, but they were nearly as dark as the walls. And he could just make out the shapes of the wooden sleepers and the rails, but he didn't like the darkness between the sleepers and between the props. If you looked at darkness like that too long you started seeing things in it: patterns, shapes, faces . . .

He listened to his father's voice. It sounded too loud, and crackly like a fire, but you could hold on to it. He was telling him about the bogeys that used to run up and down on the rails in the old days, taking the coal up to the pithead. It was good to hear his father's voice talking about the old days, but he didn't like the sound of the bogeys. He asked what a bogey was and listened as his father told him it was sort of like a railway carriage on a goods train. He knew that anyway, but he wanted to hear his father telling him again, just in case.

There were other bogeys – bogeymen. He asked if there were bogeymen down the pit. His father laughed and said that there weren't. But he knew different, he knew that it was dark enough down here for bogeymen, especially now the word had been said out loud. Bogeymen.

Sometimes if you said a word over and over again it started to sound different. It started to mean something else, to mean what it sounded like it meant. Then, if you kept on saying it over and over again, it started to not mean anything, the word started to be a thing. And the thing didn't mean anything except what it was.

He tried it now, saying it under his breath over and over again, bogeymen, bogeymen, bogeymen, bogeymen . . . But before the word could lose its meaning, his father stopped walking. He stopped too and turned, glad that they were going to go back up to the light, to the ordinary world.

'You go on,' said his father.

At first he wondered what his father meant, then he knew: he wanted him to keep on walking down into the dark. Alone. He pretended not to have heard and took a step towards the entrance of the tunnel, then he felt his father's hand on his shoulder and his heart pounding in his chest.

'Down you go,' said his father.

He didn't move. He didn't say anything, hoping his father would lose his patience with him and change his mind.

'Are you feart?' said his father.

'Naw, but . . .'

But what? He turned to the darkness. He could still see the rails and the props and the sleepers, but only just. He didn't want to see the face.

'Go on.'

He started walking down into the darkness. He had sometimes seen it in his dreams, after his father had come home late and spoken in the quiet voice to his mother about John Ireland: at first there was just the dark, the pitch-black dark that was blacker than coal, because even coal wasn't always black, because sometimes it was blue or grey, and sometimes it had a dark shine to it, like the cover of the Bible, and sometimes the coal had seams – of fool's gold, or the thin, brittle, silvery seams of mica – but the darkness in the dream had no shine to it, no seams, it was pure black. Then you felt it there like a shadow in the dark, a shadow that went long and went wide, went thick like a wall and went thin like a thread, then the shadow had the shape of a man and the man had a face and the face was the face of John Ireland.

He stopped walking, turned round and looked back at his father. He called to him and asked if he'd gone far enough.

'Further.'

It was good to hear his father's voice behind him, but it didn't last long enough to hold on to. Why didn't his father walk down further too? Why did he have to walk down on his own? Sometimes his father liked him to walk in front of him along the street. 'Walk in front,' he'd say, 'where I can see you.' Like the time he'd taken him to the gym to see John Ireland and he'd seen John Ireland's face. It looked like a bulldog's with a flattened nose and a crushed ear and big, bloodshot eyes. In the dream it looked worse. In

the dream, somehow you forgot it was the face of an old boxer. John Ireland
had given him a pair of boxing gloves. He'd tied them together and put them
round his neck on the way home. And his father had told him to walk in
front where he could see him. But that wasn't the reason, not the real reason
he wanted him to walk in front. It was because he wanted to dream about
his son being a champion boxer. He hadn't gone back to the gym because
his mother had put her foot down, but he still put the gloves on sometimes
and pretended to be a champion boxer. Now there wasn't a gym because of
what had happened at the face.

Maybe it wouldn't be like the face in his dream, but he still didn't want
to see it. He stopped and turned round. He could still see the dark shape of
his father against the light from the start of the tunnel. He shouted to him
and waited.

'Go on.'

His father's voice faded to an echo.

He turned and walked further down into the dark, the pitch-black dark
even blacker than coal, then he felt it there, a shadow in the dark . . . He
stopped, turned and shouted to his father. He could still see the dim, greyish
light from the start of the tunnel, but now he couldn't see his father. He
shouted out again. His own voice echoed and he heard the fear in it, then
all there was was the listening darkness all around and the pounding of his
heart. The shadow had the shape of a man and the man had a face . . .

As he turned to run away he was lifted in the air and his father's laughter
filled his ear. He was laughing and saying he was proud, proud of him
because he'd walked down on his own, proud because now he was a man.

He rubbed the bus window with his hand and looked out at the big, black
wheel of the pit. He watched it getting smaller as the bus pulled away, till it
was out of sight.

'Why are they gonnae shut the pit? Is there nae coal left in it?' he asked.

'There's plenty coal,' said his father, angrily.

'Why then?'

'The government wants it shut.'

'Where'll ye go tae work then?'

'Mibbe in Bilston Glen.'

'Is that another pit?'

'Aye.'

He waited a minute, then he asked, 'Has it got a face as well ?'

'Aye, it's got a face.'

'Is it like the face in your pit?'

His father shrugged. 'Much the same.'

'Ah saw it.'

'What?'

'The face.'

His father shook his head and smiled at him, the way he did when he thought he was too young to understand something.

'Ah did see it.'

'Oh ye did, did ye? What did it look like?'

'It looked like the man who ran the gym.'

And he knew he'd said something very important when his father stopped smiling, turned pale, opened his mouth to say something but didn't say anything, then stared and stared at him – as if he couldn't see him at all, but only the face of the dead man.

Fruit in season: 'The best you'll find in town' (Oscar Marzaroli)

Old man dies, George Square, Glasgow (Oscar Marzaroli)

# A Couple of Old Bigots

GEORGE FRIEL 1976

This affectionate story is set in the immediate hinterland of George Friel's native Glasgow, in some unnamed Lanarkshire coalfield village. The Protestant/Catholic sectarian divide remains strong in this part of Scotland, as the story reminds us. It is a legacy of the 19th-century Industrial Revolution and of the large influx of Ulster Catholic and Protestant families into the area.

The two miners reached the place together and Geddes lay down on the pavement. He grunted, resigned to his daily darg. Crouched on his side in an inch of water he prepared to start hewing.

'How now,' he declaimed, 'which of your hips has the most profound sciatica?'

He wriggled from his hip to his back, the pick under his right hand. Self-educated beyond his station, he liked to come out with the odd bits of Shakespeare he had learnt by heart and he got a kick out of throwing to Liam Rooney, his neighbour at the coal-face, the scraps of his unguided reading. Sometimes he did it from simple generosity, sometimes from malice aforethought. He was a quarrelsome atheist, and baiting Rooney, a practising Catholic, kept him happy. They were the best of friends.

'Tell me this, Liam,' he heaved through his toiling. 'Do you believe in free will?'

'I wish you'd give your tongue a wee rest,' Rooney complained, pushing the hutch nearer. 'You're aye blethering a lot of bloody nonsense.'

'No, but do you?' Geddes persisted. 'Damn it all, man, you surely ken what you're supposed to believe.'

'Ay, all right then, I believe in free will,' Rooney conceded. He thought the best policy was to humour Geddes, to be a willing victim and let him have his joke and his triumph. But sometimes he wished he could find an answer that Geddes couldn't use. When that ambition came to him he would make up his mind to read a book, but he never found the time and he never found the book.

'And do you believe God's almighty?' Geddes pursued him with a negroid grin.

'Of course He is,' Rooney answered impatiently. He knew there was a trap being sprung, but he couldn't see how to avoid it. 'How could He be God if He's no'?'

'But he canny be, no' if every man's got free will,' Geddes gloated up at him. 'Ye canny have it baith ways.'

'Whit way can I no'?' Rooney demanded.

Geddes kept it up, but it led nowhere. At the end of the shift they left the place together and walked one behind the other the couple of miles to the cage. They were working at the furthest point from the main road and lagged a fair distance behind the other miners. Then Geddes stopped suddenly, his hand out to stop Rooney too. They heard a creaking in the pine props, but they weren't sure where it came from.

'Go on!' Rooney screamed, pushing Geddes forward.

'No, get back,' Geddes shouted, shoving Rooney the other way.

The speed of his turn threw him off balance and he finished up sprawling across Rooney just as the first of the fall came down. It cut them off from the rest of the shift, and it was all over in less than a minute. The tumult was like a tenement collapsing, like thunder directly overhead.

'Jesus, Mary and Joseph!' Rooney panted, blessing himself. He gawked up at the threatening roof. The roar of its anger stopped, and there was only an occasional belch as some fragments shifted, a mild pattering as the soil filtered through.

'I wonder how long that's been pickling,' Geddes muttered resentfully. 'They ought to have kent aboot that.'

Rooney squatted on his hunkers, gulping and mouthing. He wanted to speak, to ask questions that Geddes would answer encouragingly since Geddes was the clever one with an answer to everything, but he couldn't get a word out.

'How much of it fell do you think?' Geddes asked him.

'A hell of a lot by the sound of it,' Rooney whispered, really frightened.

They were three and a half days in there together and stuck it out well because they were old friends, though Rooney lost his temper twice. The first time was when Geddes laughed at him for taking out his rosary and saying Our Fathers and Hail Marys on and on, mysteriously.

'Christ, dae ye aye carry thae beads wi' ye?' he scoffed.

'Ye ken damn fine I aye have my rosary in my pocket,' Rooney snapped. 'And ye could do worse than say a wee prayer yourself.'

The second time he lost his temper was half-way through the second day when Geddes was seized with a sudden spasm of vigour and hammered too near the bone.

'Ay, but to die, and go we know not where.

To lie in cold obstruction and to rot.'

'Ach, shut yer face,' Rooney growled. 'We're no' a' that deid yet.'

To begin with they did what they could to clear away the rubble, cheering each other, keeping their spirits up with guessing-games, football quizzes and songs. Geddes sang 'The Star o' Rabbie Burns' and Rooney taught him 'Faith of Our Fathers'. They drank the moisture that dripped from the roof, but long before they were rescued they were too weak to move. They were silent for hours at a stretch, past singing and arguing. The knocking they had answered over the nightmare term of darkness came slowly nearer and they sat against the wall and waited.

'Are ye all right, Liam?' Geddes croaked.

'Ay, I'm grand, Willie,' Rooney breathed faintly.

'It'll no be lang noo,' Geddes comforted him. 'Ay, we'll be having a pint in Sloan's the morrow night, you and me, so we will.'

The first small gap appeared. They heard voices come through loud and clear. They got a glimpse of Lumsden, the brusher, and the wall-eye of Grant the drawer. Then a large anonymous hand came to them with food and drink.

It wasn't the first accident they were in, and it wasn't the last, but it was the only time they were alone together. It was one more bond between them. They went back to work on the same day, still neighbours on the same shift, and their dialogue went on as before.

'Willie Geddes has got some terrible stories about the Popes,' Rooney told his wife. 'I don't know where he gets the half of them. But if he's right there's been some quare old birds in the Vatican.'

'Sure everybody knows there's been bad Popes,' Mrs Rooney shrugged it off, ladling out his soup. 'You don't need Willie Geddes to tell you that.'

'Well, he's told me one or two things I never knew,' Rooney said grudgingly. 'Then he says, Ay, and you believe the Pope's infallible!'

His daughter looked up perkily from her secondary school homework spread out at the other end of the kitchen table and gave him advice.

'Just you tell him the Church doesn't say the Pope's impeccable.'

Her father glowered at her, ready to be embarrassed by the implications of the strange word. She explained it.

'Jees, I'll catch him with that one tomorrow,' he laughed. 'That's a rare word that is.'

The next time Geddes got on to the lives of the Popes Rooney carefully repeated what his daughter told him.

'Have you been reading a book?' Geddes asked sourly.

'Och, I don't need to be reading books,' Rooney joked. 'I learned a thing or two at school. Of course an Orangeman like you canny understand Catholic doctrine.'

'I'm no' an Orangeman,' Geddes shouted, angry at the name. 'I read the Freethinker every week, as you damn well know.'

'Well you ought to be,' Rooney cut back at him. 'Sure your father was, and his father afore him.'

'Keep my father out of it,' Geddes huffed. 'I know a lot mair aboot religion than a bigot like you.'

'I'm no' a bigot,' Rooney protested. 'It's you that's the bigot.'

'It's no', it's you,' Geddes insisted. 'You'll never admit you're in the wrong.'

'I will so, if I am,' Rooney retorted. 'It's you that's always sure you're right.'

It went on like that for years, and as they spent their days in familiar disputation old age came along and joined them, making in their company a third of whose presence they were only slowly aware. They became old grey men, they qualified for their pension, they stopped working, they mooned about the dying mining village, they drank together in Sloan's, and Geddes always got on to religion. The retreating years were making Rooney more devout, and more touchy in his piety, but they were making Geddes more aggressive, as if he had to prove his case to Rooney before it was too late and death proved everything.

They were two dottering old men, two local worthies, and the village smiled on their crabbit friendship and loved them equally. They might have gone to their common end still friends if Geddes hadn't said too much in Sloan's one Saturday night with a good drink on him. He dragged in the Virgin Mary and spoke of her with a coarseness he had never used before. He had been clever and sarcastic, he had been jocular and irreverent, but never coarse. Rooney was shocked. He was hurt. He looked into his pint and shook his head over it.

'That's enough, Willie,' he said. 'Maybe you're my best friend, but that's just wicked blasphemy. You've went too far this time. You're just an old bigot, so you are. I'm finished wi' ye!'

He emptied his glass and left the bar without another word, neither hurriedly nor slowly, walking out quite calmly.

'Christ almighty, some people!' Geddes complained to the barman. 'Canny take a joke.'

He had another drink to cover his vexation.

'He's no' getting me to go running after him,' he told the neutral barman. 'Him and his Virgin Mary! I don't believe a word of it.'

He waited for Rooney to come back and be teased into conversation again. He waited till the bar closed, and then he had to plod home alone. Over the next few days he tried to find Rooney. He went to all the usual places at the usual times, but he never saw him. His wife, coming in from her shopping, would tell him she had just seen Rooney here or there, all by himself, and he acknowledged the information with a grunt. He didn't want to tell her Rooney was deliberately avoiding him. He brooded, sour in his loneliness.

He didn't have to brood long. Rooney died in his sleep a week later, when a January wind was bringing a sleet across the village. He was in his chair at the fireside when his wife bustled in with the news.

'I just met Mrs Lumsden in the grocer's there,' she said. 'She was telling me Liam Rooney passed away during the night.'

'Och ay,' he nodded with Scottish brevity, showing no emotion.

He sat forward in his chair, staring into the fire, and as he looked at the living coals he thought of the pit. Nearly sixty years of working with Rooney jumbled through his mind, and the fire was refracted through his unfallen tears. When he went for his afternoon walk memories of Rooney kept him company. He was passing Sloan's when a young woman crossed the street to speak to him. It was Miss Rooney, teacher of modern languages in the local Catholic secondary school.

'Oh, Willie,' she said, very grave, 'You'll have heard about my father?'

'Oh ay,' he said solemnly, and waited.

'I was on my way round to see you.' Rooney's daughter spoke to him softly. 'My mother sent me. She wants you to take a cord.'

'But that's no' my place, that's for the nearest,' Geddes said, his scalp prickling at the very thought of going to a Catholic funeral. 'And there's all your uncles.'

'Oh, you come before any of them,' she warmed him with a wee smile. 'Some of them have never put a foot across the door for years. You were the first my mother mentioned when she was asked who was all taking a cord.'

'Your mother's very kind,' he said.

He went to see the widow. He guessed at once Rooney had never told her of their last night at the bar. She had no idea her husband's last days on earth were spent avoiding his old butty. He said what he could to show his sympathy, and she gave him hers.

'It was that sudden, Willie,' she whimpered. 'And you'll miss him yourself. After all these years. You and him were through the General Strike thegither and on till that November, and that wasn't yesterday. And he thought the world of you. Every time he came off a shift it was Willie Geddes says this and Willie Geddes says that. Just the night before he died he was talking about you.'

'But how can I go to the funeral?' he asked, screwing up his eyes. 'Me in a Catholic church! They wouldn't let me in, would they? You know what I am.'

'Now you've no call to be worrying about that,' Mrs Rooney smacked his hand lightly. 'God knows best what we all are. If you think you'd feel strange coming into the church just you meet the party at the door when they bring the body out. All I want you to do is take a cord when they lower the coffin —'

She started to cry again, her own words too blunt for her, and his huge hand patted her shoulder.

'I know Liam would have wanted you there,' she sniffled.

He put on a black tie and his good suit and his dark coat and he went to the funeral. He stood beside the grave while a chubby priest, talking Latin with a Donegal accent, said a lot of prayers he couldn't follow, and when he had taken the cord assigned to him and helped to lower the coffin deep into the damp clay he saw the priest sprinkle water on the lid with a little feather duster. Stuck at the edge of the dismal pit, he felt he was a white man taking part in the rites of a black tribe. On the other side of the grave four of Rooney's unknown brothers, big men with heavy coats and dull faces, huddled together and their lips moved knowingly to the priest's last prayer.

When they stopped praying they made the sign of the cross, and determined to be just as much Liam Rooney's mourner as any of them, old Geddes too made the sign of the cross. At that moment he remembered a phrase he had often heard Rooney use, and he repeated it deliberately in a willing suspension of his disbelief.

'God rest him,' he mumbled.

The wind across the cemetery crested his white hair, slapped at the tails of his coat and chilled his old bones.

# Silver Linings

JOAN LINGARD 1986

This is a first-person narrative in which Sam tells her own energetic story. The tatty city street full of second-hand and nearly-new shops is based on St Stephen's Street, in Edinburgh's New Town. As the story says, it's not a bit like the more upmarket Princes Street where all the tourists go. But it has its own promise and its own excitements – and its own moral dilemmas.

Every cloud is supposed to have one, or so I learned at my granny's knee. Isn't that where you're supposed to learn such things? My granny is full of sayings, most of them rubbish, according to my mother, who has her own sayings. Like most mothers. My granny isn't one of those grandmothers who sits and knits in the chimney corner, shrouded in shawls, if such grannies exist at all. She tints her hair auburn and is employed as manageress at a local supermarket. It's not all that 'super', I must add, as it's only got two aisles, one up and one down, but still, a job's a job these days. And money doesn't grow . . .

Money's a problem in our family and my granny helps keep us afloat with 'care' parcels. She dumps them down on the kitchen table muttering about the improvidence of my parents and the wasted education of my mother who had all the chances in life that she didn't have herself. Etcetera. My father is not a lot of use when it comes to providing. He does odd jobs and he comes and goes. Like driftwood, says my granny, who doesn't understand what her daughter saw in him.

I think it was probably his name. He's called Torquil. My mother's got a thing about names. Her own given name was Isobel. A good plain no-nonsense Scottish Christian name. The only person who uses it now is my granny. My mother is known to everyone else as Isabella or Bella.

My name is Samantha, which my mother uses in full, but my friends call me Sam and my brother's called Seb, short for Sebastian. My granny approves of neither the short nor the long versions. 'Sam and Seb – sounds like two cartoon characters!' She hates having to introduce us, it gives her a 'red face'. She had wanted us to be called Jean and Colin. So she calls me hen and Seb, son.

The legendary Madam Doubtfire and her trusty cat. Not so long ago, they presided over a nearly-new basement shop in Edinburgh, just around the corner from Sam and Seb. (Douglas Corrance)

Anyway, to get back to silver linings. I don't know about clouds having them but for a short time we had in our possession a fur coat which had one. But, first, I'd better explain about my mother's shop.

She keeps a second-hand clothes shop in a street that's full of shops selling second-hand things, from books to old fenders and clocks to medals and feather boas (though they're scarce) and silk petticoats (usually full of snaps and runs) and woollens (usually washed in). There are also two or three bars in the street, and some cafés. We like it, Seb and I. There's always something going on. The shop's in a basement (a damp one) across the road from our flat. You can doubtless imagine what my granny thinks of it. She says the smell of the old clothes turns her stomach and folk that buy stuff like that need their heads examined.

But people do come in and buy, not that it's ever like the shops in Princes Street on a Saturday. And they tend to sit on boxes and blether to my mother for hours before they get round to buying some ghastly looking dress with a V neck and a drooping hemline that was fashionable during the war. And then they find they haven't got quite enough money to pay for it so my mother says she'll get it from them the next time they're in. You can see why we need the care parcels.

When my mother goes out on the rummage for new stock – new old stock, that is – she just shuts up the shop and leaves a note on the door saying 'Back in ten minutes' or, if I'm home from school, she leaves me in charge with my friend Morag. (Nice name, Morag, says my granny.) Morag and I amuse ourselves by trying on the clothes and parading up and down like models. We usually have a good laugh too. I like long traily dresses in black crêpe de chine and big floppy hats and Morag likes silks and satins. We don't bother with the washed-in woollies.

One day my mother came back in a taxi filled to bursting with old clothes. She was bursting with excitement too, even gave the taxi driver a pound tip. You'd have thought we were about to make our fortune!

Morag and I helped to haul in the catch. We sat on the floor in the middle of it and unpacked the bags. There were dresses of every colour of the rainbow, made of silk and of satin, of brocade and of very fine wool.

'They belonged to an old lady,' said my mother.

The dresses smelt really old when you pressed them to your face.

'She died last month.'

We shivered a little and let the dresses fall into our laps.

'She was *very* old though.'

We cheered up and turned our attention to the blouses and scarves and the satin shoes. The old lady must never have thrown anything away.

And then out of a bag I took a fur coat. Now my mother doesn't like fur coats, usually won't handle them. By that, I mean sell them. She's for Beauty Without Cruelty. As I am myself. But this coat felt kind of smooth and silky, even though it was a bit bald looking here and there, and so I slipped it on.

'I'll have to get rid of that quickly,' said my mother.

I stroked the fur.

'Poor animal,' said my mother.

I slipped my hands into the pockets. I was beginning to think there was something funny about the coat. The lining felt odd, sort of lumpy, and I thought I could hear a faint rustling noise coming from inside it. I took the coat off.

The lining had been mended in a number of places by someone who could sew very fine stitches. I lifted the scissors and quickly began to snip the thread.

'What are you doing that for?' asked my mother irritably.

'Wait!'

I eased my hand up between the lining and the inside of the coat and brought out a five pound note. Morag gasped. And then I brought out another and another and then a ten pound one and then another five and a ten –

'I don't believe it!' said my mother, who looked as pale as the off-white blouse she was crumpling between her hands.

We extracted from the lining of the coat one thousand and ten pounds in old bank notes. They were creased and aged, but they were real enough. We sat in silence and stared at them. My mother picked up a ten pound note and peered at it in the waning afternoon light.

'She can't have trusted the bank. Old people are sometimes funny that way. Keep their money in mattresses and places.' Like old coats.

'We could go for a holiday,' I said.

'A Greek island,' murmured my mother. 'Paros. Or Naxos.'

Once upon a time she used to wander around islands, with my father, before Seb and I were born. I could see us, the three of us, lying on the warm sand listening to the soft swish of the blue blue sea.

'Are you going to keep it?' asked Morag, breaking into our trance. She's a bit like that, Morag, down-to-earth, a state of being that my granny is fully in favour of.

My mother bit the side of her lip, the way she does when she's a bit confused. She quite often bites her lip.

'Finder's keepers,' I said hopefully. Hadn't my granny taught me that?

'I did *pay* for the coat.'

Not a thousand pounds of course, we knew that.

'Who did you buy it from?' asked Morag.

'A relative of the old lady's. He was clearing out the house. He looked well enough heeled.'

'In that case –' I said.

'I'll need to think about it,' said my mother. 'In the meantime –' She glanced about her and I got up to put on the light and draw the curtains.

What *were* we to do with the money?

'We could sew it back into the coat,' I suggested.

That seemed as good an idea as any other so Morag and I pushed the notes back into the lining, all but one ten pound one which my mother said we might as well keep out to buy something for supper with that evening.

'Morag,' she said, sounding a bit awkward, 'don't be saying anything about this to anyone else eh?'

'I wouldn't dream of it, Isabella.' (My mother likes my friends to call her by her Christian name. She likes Seb and me to do it too but when I'm talking about her I always refer to her as 'my mother'.)

When I chummed Morag along the street on her way home I told her I'd kill her if she did tell and we almost quarrelled as she said I'd no business to doubt her word. But it was such a big secret to keep! I felt choked up with the excitement of it.

We took the fur coat across the road with us when we went home and over an Indian carry-out and a bottle of rosé wine my mother and Seb and I discussed the problem of whether we were entitled to keep the money or not. Seb and I thought there was no problem at all.

'You bought the coat, Bella,' said Seb. 'Everything in it's yours.'

'Well, I don't know. Maybe, legally, but morally . . . I mean, I suppose I *should* give it back.'

'But you want to go to Greece don't you?' I said.

Her lip trembled.

Outside, it was raining. Big heavy drops were striking the window pane and the wind was making the glass rattle in its frame.

'You could both be doing with new shoes,' said our mother. 'Mind you, with money like that . . .' She sighed.

The next day was Saturday. We took the coat back over to the shop with us in the morning, afraid to let it out of our sight. My mother put it in a cupboard in the back room where she keeps garments that are waiting to be mended. Some are beyond redemption but they wait nevertheless.

In the afternoon, we had to go to a family wedding, on my father's side. My father was supposed to be there. My mother and I kitted ourselves out with clothes from the shop.

'Well, honestly!' declared my granny, on her arrival. She was to mind the shop while we were gone. 'I could have lent you a nice wee suit, Isobel.' She turned to look me over. 'Do you think black crêpe de chine's the right thing to be wearing at a wedding? And at your age too!' She didn't even call me hen. She couldn't have thought I looked endearing. The dress had come out of the old lady's wardrobe.

In the bus, Seb said to our mother, 'Now don't tell Father about the money if he *is* there.'

He did turn up. He was his usual 'charming' self, never stuck for words. I was pleased enough to see him to begin with but after a bit when I saw him sweet-talking our mother and her cheeks beginning to turn pink and her eyes lighting up, I felt myself going off him. Seb and I sat side by side and drank as much fizzy wine as we could get hold of and listened to her laugh floating down the room.

'She'll tell him,' said Seb gloomily.

She did of course. And he decided to come home with us. They walked in front of us holding hands.

'When will she ever learn?' said Seb, sounding strangely like our granny.

'Good evening, Torquil,' said that lady very stiffly, when we came into the shop where she was sitting playing Clock Patience on the counter top. 'Stranger,' she couldn't resist adding.

'Hi, Ma!' He gave her a smacking kiss on the cheek. 'It's good to see you. You're not looking a day older.'

She did not return the compliment.

'Been busy?' asked my mother.

'Not exactly rushed off my feet. I sold two or three dresses and one of those tatty Victorian nightgowns – oh, and yon moth-eaten fur coat in the cupboard through the back.'

She might just as well have struck us all down with a sledgehammer. We were in a state of total collapse for at least five minutes until my mother managed to get back the use of her tongue.

'You sold *that coat?*'

'Well, why not? You hate having fur lying around.'

'Who did you sell it to?' My mother was doing her best to stay calm.

'How should I know? Some woman. She came in asking if we'd any furs. She gave me twenty pounds for it. I didn't think you could ask a penny more. Lucky to get that.'

My mother told my granny about the money in the lining and then it was her turn to collapse. I thought we were going to have to call a doctor to revive her. My father managed it with some brandy that he had in his coat pocket.

'Oh no,' she moaned, 'oh *no*. But what did you leave it in the shop for, Isobel?'

'It was in the back shop! In the cupboard.'

They started to argue, to blame one another. Seb and I went out and roamed the streets till dark and long after looking for the woman in our fur coat. We never did see it again.

Our father left the next morning.

'Shows him up for what he is, doesn't it?' said our granny. 'He only came back for the money. He'd have taken you to the cleaners, Isobel. Maybe it was just as well. As I always say –'

She stopped.

Not even she had the nerve to look my mother in the eye and say that every cloud has its silver lining.

Boy, Gorbals, Glasgow (Oscar Marzaroli)

# The Bit about Growing

BESS ROSS 1995

This is a contemporary story about families and neighbours, and how they relate to one another and respect one another. A young boy learns about life from an old man. Wherever you live, growing up is about learning to cope with all the things that get in the way. And wherever you live, these things are much the same. Bess Ross writes about her own home background – Easter Ross.

'Hand that bit there up to me.' The Grilse pointed to the pile of driftwood lying stacked in the corner of his shed. It was the back end of the year and he was working on his boat. He had a mind to have her down in the spring.

Neil looked at the heap. He hadn't a clue which piece the worn, bent finger was pointing to.

'Is it this bit?' he chanced and handed a stout board to the old man.

'Ay, that one.' He took the wood from Neil. 'Come here and hold it for me.' He placed the plank on the horsey, lifted his saw from the bench. The veins on the backs of his hands were a network of knotted rope. Neil pressed down hard on the wood with both hands, ensuring that it did not slip.

'Ay, like that. Keep her steady.' The saw whistled and wobbled as it tore through the soft bleached wood.

Neil watched as the old man walked over to his boat, measured the cut wood for size. He was glad to be away from his house; there was always some bawling going on. Between Jo and his mother mostly. Or Jo and his father. Like today.

Jo had risen late, no one was allowed to open their mouths the mood he was in. The usual morning-after story. He turned off whatever obscure programme their father had been staring at and fed his Schwarzenegger tape into the video. And that was when hell broke out. It ended with Jo slamming from the house, doing his best to take the door with him, and shattering its glass in the process. When Neil left the house some minutes later Jo was sitting in the greenhouse glowering at the sad geraniums, his foot tormenting the cat.

'Jo says he's going to Australia.' Neil spoke to The Grilse's back.

'Hm.' The Grilse straightened, turned from his joinery to face Neil. 'The wandering ones. That's what they used to call us. That's Jo I'm thinking. This bit's no use.' He walked back to the woodpile, tossed the discarded wood on the top then began raking through it for a more suitable piece. Neil stood in the sawdust and watched him.

'His feet's itchy.' He found what he was looking for and Neil's eyes followed him back to the boat. He walked slowly, his feet dragging on the shed floor. It was as if an invisible wire was stretched tight between his forehead and his toes forcing his head and shoulders down, restricting his footsteps.

'My mother says she's putting the flag up when he goes.'

'Ach, that's your mother's tongue speaking. If I know your mother she'll have the pipe band out for him when he comes home. Catch that other bit for me like a good fellow, the bit we had,' and Neil hurried to obey.

'Myself was sixteen when I left home for the first time,' The Grilse spoke through a mouthful of nails. 'The first time I went anywhere it was to Glasgow to get a ship.'

'What, you were only here till then?'

'Different days, Neil boy.' He tapped a nail home. 'I went into the town once before that, walked in and walked out. Twelve miles each time. I had to go for the doctor for Old Mailey's teeth. The doctor pulled teeth in them days, there wasn't a dentist in it.'

Neil found it hard to imagine what it would be like growing up in the village when The Grilse was young. Never going anywhere. He'd been to Orkney with the school in second year. Last year they went to France, in primary they went to London, visited the houses of Parliament, met their MP and were on *Jim'll Fix It*. His Mam taped that; they still had it.

'It was, as you might say, a rude awakening.' The Grilse's voice brought him back.

'I think my mother's worried about Jo.'

'Surely she is, she's his mother. Are you keeping that right?'

Neil readjusted his hold on the plank. The Grilse's shed was filled with sea things. Lobster pots lay about in various stages of disrepair, dark-green glass floats rolled on the bench and caught the light from the window; his driftwood took up every corner, and then there was rope. Of every thickness. Blue rope, orange rope, white rope, dark-brown ropey rope, which smelled of oil and the sea. In the middle of all this lay his boat, her keel in the air, a gaping hole in her side exposing her bones.

'Tell your mother that I'm telling her she's no to be worrying about Jo. Jo's alright. He'll take care of himself. Yourself'll miss him though, I'm thinking,' and the look he gave Neil was keen.

'Not me. I hate all the fighting.'

'Fighting! What's fighting? Is that no families?' and he took hold of Neil's end. His aim was still sure, he didn't miss a nail once.

'I better be going now. My dinner'll be ready.'

'Right you are then. Will you come back?' He didn't turn from his work.

'Ay, okay,' and Neil walked away from the ramshackle old shed, made out of wood and corrugated tin with a house window in the side. The tap-tap-tapping of The Grilse's hammer followed him.

Peace had broken out by the time Neil returned home. As he put his head in the door only the disembodied sounds of the television set met him. Jo was back, sitting on the settee, his back straight. Too straight. His face looked softer after the fight, not quite so girny. His hair was beginning to grow back in. Two weeks before he'd had what was left removed for a double vodka bet. Some guys could look really hard cases with a skinhead haircut. Jo only succeeded in looking vulnerable.

'Where were you anyway, as if I need to ask?' he barked at Neil. There was nothing soft about his tone.

'If you know so much why are you asking then?' Neil threw himself down into an armchair, retrieved *The Beano* from beneath its cushion.

'Don't start,' their father said.

'What stuff's The Grilse filling your head with now?' Jo carried on, his long legs stretched before him waiting to trip somebody.

'Nothing.' Neil's head was in his comic.

'Ay, right enough, that's about the size of it,' and Jo's left foot shot out to hook *The Beano* from Neil's hands.

Their father sighed loudly and threw them a heavy look.

Neil picked up his comic and went back to his reading.

'You listen to all that guff,' Jo needled.

'It is not guff.' Neil's eyes never strayed from the page: 'He knows plenty.'

'He's living in another century. "I remember when I was your age . . ." '

Jo affected a thin shaky voice. 'What does he know about anything anyway, old geek?' and his left foot began to nark at Neil's right ankle.

'He knows,' Neil said, moving his feet. 'Why do you think he left here when he was sixteen?' His voice was ringing, colour flushed his face.

'Where did he go to? To Inverness?' Jo scoffed.

'Well, smart Alec if you want to know, he left to join the navy. He saw everywhere.'

'Who? Him? That old shape? Is that true?' Jo turned to his father.

'I don't know,' his father said. 'Yes, I think so.'

'And I bet he didn't make as big a noise as you about going,' Neil said and he drove a vicious kick at Jo's ankle. 'Lay off, will you. Get a life.'

'Cut it, the pair of you,' their father shouted.

'What's The Grilse's real name anyway?' Jo asked him some minutes later when all was quiet once more.

'I don't know. John Mackay I think. The same as yourself. He's related to us somewhere. Ask your mam. She'll know.'

Jo pressed his lips together and thought on that. The old guy!

'And you can get that homework of yours done,' their father shouted at Neil, his concentration on the television momentarily broken. 'Everything left until the last minute as usual. Do you want to end up nowhere too?'

'He's going to end up there anyway,' Jo's laugh was derisory. 'What's in this place for anyone? In this country? Zilch!' He was up on his soapbox again.

An indistinguishable mumble floated through the open door from the kitchen as their mother fought and lost in the battle of the water taps and the television set.

'Just because you mucked things up.' Neil kept his head down and his grip firm.

'Who mucked it up?' Jo demanded. 'I could be anything.'

'Ay, but your problem, Jo, is you don't want to be anything. You make me sick. All I ever heard, all my life, was how clever you were and how couldn't I be like you? Now look at you! Five Highers and a heap of Standard grades and all you do is drift around with that lot.'

Neil was edging it and he knew it. He cleared his feet well away from Jo's firing line, tucked his head into his shoulders.

'Ay, ay, we all know where you'd be. Circumnavigating the globe like Vasco da Gama.'

'One thing I wouldn't be and that's stuck in a shed all day.'

In the silence that followed Neil heard only his own words ringing. Jo's face had fallen in on him, his lower lip sagged. No one had to tell him anything about standing on concrete all day cutting steel, feet crying, choked with the fumes from the paint shop. On the back shift never seeing the summer nights, in winter the stars. And not being able to find a sleep pattern. Under the stubble haircut he looked about four years old.

'Other people go to university, but not you, never you. You're so special of course.' Neil wouldn't leave it.

'University! University! That's all I ever hear. From everybody. You can't move in this place without someone going on at you. "You're still here, Jo. I thought you'd be off to the university by now." Is university the world?' The walls were rocking to the volume of his voice. 'I'm never going to want what they have. People telling me how to think. Will university make me play for the Washington Redskins? Will university show me where the universe ends? Just quit it, will you?' and he leapt for the door. The house held its breath as it waited for the walls to come crashing down.

'I'm getting out of here if it's the last thing I do,' he announced after one of his weekends. At nineteen his life was going nowhere, and he was beginning to realise it.

'What am I meant to do? Sit in at night with my mammy and my daddy. I'm sick of driving about on my own looking for something happening. The only thing that's happening is me, racing the Thurso train. I'm out of it.'

That was when Australia came up. It was easier than the States, you didn't need a permit. You could go out on a year's holiday visa. That was for him. The States – one day, he said.

'Promises, promises,' they all said.

'You'll be sorry,' Jo shouted.

The Grilse's breath came from him in short sharp gasps. He struggled for it, his chest felt as tight as a drum. He raked among nails in an old syrup tin, selected a few of the kind he was looking for.

'You'll soon have her finished,' Neil spoke from the open door of the shed. He looked at the old man's repair. It wasn't very good. He'd used differing thicknesses of wood on the hole. And they were nailed on squint. The ends of some of his boards were torn where he'd snapped them with his foot. New wood was nailed on to old.

'Ay, a coat of tar over that and she'll be sound. As tight as a kettle. What do you say?' and he stood beside Neil to assess his work.

'Ay,' Neil said. 'No bad.'

'I'll paint her later. Mary'll chase me if she'll find me even looking at paint with this chest.'

'This blue here,' he walked over to the bench, clapped a hand to a large tin, 'and this white.' He reached far back on the bench and pulled the white forward to sit beside the blue. 'I'll do that later, if all's well,' and he stood that way awhile, stooped over the workbench, his hands cupping the two tins of paint.

'I don't know, my chest's that tight,' he spoke as if to himself as he shuffled over to the broken chair, lowered himself carefully on to it, his claw hand clasping his sharp knees. He tried to clear something from his throat but could not.

'I hope you're no going to that place,' he said to Neil when he'd given up on whatever was obstructing his gullet.

'Eh? What?' Neil was sitting on an upended lobster pot, staring through the open door to the shore.

'When I was over at the shop. Getting the rolls and the newspaper. Two men were talking,' he spoke between the gasps. 'There's a house in this village. Boys are going in to it. They're at the drugs,' he wheezed. There was nothing wrong with his ears.

'Well, you needn't be looking at me,' Neil flared, his face as red as his hair.

'I hope not.'

'Well you can hope, because I don't. Honest. I'd be too scared anyway.'

'And what about Jo?'

'Are you wise? Jo would never touch anything. He even hates fags. I know some of those boys. Two are in my year. Deadbeats!' and Neil was back to studying rock and shore.

'Dirty things!' The Grilse found what was lying in his chest, spat it on the floor.

'Well, you needn't look at me,' Neil repeated and the toe of his right trainer made patterns in the stour.

'Bad things,' the old man went on as if Neil hadn't spoken.

'Tell me something I don't know,' Neil said. The Grilse could be funny when he liked, Jo wasn't all wrong there.

'You'll be thinking that I'm an old gowk.' Neil jumped at the words. The old fellow could see inside him!

'No, I'm not. I don't.' He erased the patterns, began on new ones.

'I had all that thrown at me when I was not much above your own age. And I didn't have the comfort of my home at my back. Nothing new there.'

'Did you ever try anything?" Neil stopped his drawing, looked closely at the old man.

'No sir! Never!' He lapsed into quietness and Neil thought that was the end of it.

'What's in them? Now, ask yourself that?' and he thrust a bony forefinger Neil's way.

Neil shrugged his shoulders. 'I don't know.'

'No more do I. But whatever it is that's in them, it can't do anyone any good. That you may be sure of.'

Neil said nothing to this. There was no point. The Grilse was off. If his shortness of breath wouldn't stop him then neither would anything that Neil might say.

'How old would you say that I am? Look at me now,' and the voice was strong enough.

'I don't know,' Neil said again, not wanting to risk offending him by saying something foolish.

'If all's well I'll be eighty-five years on the tenth of January. And the more that I know, the less I know, if you know what I mean.'

Neil didn't. He hadn't a clue.

'But one thing I have learned and it's this. Inside every one of us is everything that we'll ever need. If we're lucky enough to have our health. All inside us here, Neil,' and he tapped his spare chest with a forefinger. 'Look at yourself now, bonnie with it too. Just like myself,' and he cackled like a hen, clapped a tattoo on his knees.

Oh ay, Neil thought, I wish. A head like a coconut, a lump of steel in my mouth and now spots.

'Don't ever tamper with what'll harm you,' the old man was serious again. 'Look at me now. Are you hearing what I'm saying to you?'

Neil looked at the opal eyes. He had to force himself not to burst out laughing at the fierce old face looking back at him.

'It's easy enough to die. We all do sometime. Anyone can do it. But how we live, Neil boy. That's a different story. Are you hearing now?'

'Ay,' Neil said, fiddling with the collar of his jacket. Cripes, the old fellow was getting awful heavy.

'Do you have a girl in that school of yours?' he asked, changing tack.

'No chance,' Neil's face was a beetroot. He squirmed on the lobster pot as he felt the embarrassment take him.

'And what about Jo? Is he courting?'

'Him? Never! There's no one perfect enough for him. There's always girls on the phone but he can't be bothered. He says he's looking for someone like himself.'

The Grilse opened his mouth in a wide gummy smile, shook his head. 'I'm thinking he's going to have some search then. But mind,' the smile slipped from him, 'she'll be a very special lassie when he finds her.'

'There's no such person. That's what my mam says. Not in the whole world. Can't be, she says. Imagine a female Jo. Doc Martens, a bad attitude and a bald head.'

'Like myself,' The Grilse chipped in.

'Ugh!' Neil's hands went to his throat, he pretended to faint from the thought. And the tin walls of The Grilse's shed reverberated to their wild laughter.

'Mind you, we saw all kinds in the navy. Ach, you saw everything. When I was not much older than yourself is. There was nothing in it for us then but to go to the sea. What else could we do? You got to know the fellows making the same trip. Sometimes you'd meet up with them in Montreal and Auckland and Valparaiso, Curaçao, places like that. Different places. You'd always meet someone you knew.' The old voice softened, grew thin. 'The best friend that I had when I was in the navy came from the Island of Eriskay. A lot of the island men joined the fleet. Davy MacLennan his name was. Fine man. Oh yes.'

Neil looked up at the old man's face. He didn't know what he saw written there. He looked away.

'Big, big fellow. Strong. Like a bull. He'd play anything on the mouth organ. His favourite was "The Eriskay Love Lilt". Do you know it?' and he began to croon something below his breath.

Neil shook his head. It was hard to tell whether he did or not. The Grilse's humming was practically soundless, totally tuneless.

'He'd play "The Hilltown Fishers" to me. Now, you know that one?'

'Ay, my granda used to sing it. My mam still does.'

'Good for her. We buried Davy in the South Pacific Sea. He got hit on the head with a hook from a crane. Ay,' and he shook his head again, the way a dog does, as if he would shake the memory from him. He rose from the chair, walked over to the bench, began rearranging the tins of paint, gathering up and sorting the loose lying nails.

'How was he called The Grilse anyway?' Jo asked his father on the day that the village heard of the old man's passing. He had died four days into his eighty-sixth year. It was his lungs, they whispered in the shop. What had begun as 'flu carried him up to the cemetery.

'I'm not sure,' his father said. 'Ask your mam. She'll know.'

'Well,' Jo's mother told him, 'Granda told me it was because he used to go out with the salmon-fishers when he was a wee bairn. And you know what a grilse is, a young salmon. He was at the salmon-fishing on and off all his life, whenever he came home from the sea. A *carnhar* like Granda was.' She paused, looked to one, then the other. 'Where's Neil?' she asked.

'Through in his room,' they said.

Neil couldn't believe it. The Grilse had died awful quick. He said he was going to paint the boat. And he was dead. It wasn't fair. Neil screwed his eyes shut to try to stop the tears coming. He thumped his pillow as he fought for control. It just wasn't fair. Silly old fool, who did he think he was anyway? Dying just like that. Just going off without saying even one word. To anybody. 'Anyone can die, anyone can die,' Neil wanted to rip the words out of his head. His fists were pistons and his pillow was there. All the helplessness, the rawness, the lostness and the utter confusion that was choking him spewed from his fists. 'Anyone can die, anyone can die.' Big deal. Who cared? Neil flung himself across his bed and howled.

Later he was able to see clearly. He was walking along the shore one day, doing nothing, when he found he could look up at the shed without experiencing the red hot dagger in his chest. He wasn't sure what it was that he did feel, but whatever it was the cruel crippling pain was gone.

'It's how we live,' he had said. And once, 'To live is to grow. If we don't do that, what then, Neil boy? We'd be as well to be dead. Huh!'

Jo was in Sydney and they all missed him most terribly. Their days had a different shade of light without Jo. His father made a small noise about the reversed charge phone calls. But his mother didn't care. All she and Neil wanted was to hear Jo's voice. His father too. His mother swung between euphoria when Jo phoned or when a letter arrived from Australia to dark despair in between, convinced the whole of Australia was waiting solely to harm him.

Neil loved Jo. How could he ever have thought that he hated him? When he wasn't being aggravating and narky, Jo was ace. He wrote good long letters to Neil. He told him that the hardest thing that he had ever done was to get on the train at Inverness and not get straight back off again. And Sydney was a beautiful city. So clean, so much going on. All the time. And, oh Neil, you should see the nights.

In Sydney, eleven thousand miles from his home Jo would be doing his growing. As the time for his leaving had drawn closer and it dawned on his mother that he really was going, she nearly flipped. Yes, she did hear him right. He was going all that way on his own. And no, he didn't want any addresses. Of anyone. Unless she knew Crocodile Dundee. Being Jo he'd do it his way.

'He said that you were to have *The Puffin*,' Mary, The Grilse's daughter, said to Neil as they left the house on the day of the funeral. Neil couldn't look at Mary's face; he left his mother and father to do the talking. Back then he didn't want to know about anything.

He stopped his walking, looked up at the shed again. It stood out from the neat concrete squares of its neighbours. The Grilse's shed was different. Like he himself had been different. Like Jo was. Jo like an old shed! Neil's grin was wide at the thought. He picked up a stone, pitched it far out into the waves. He must tell him that one when he wrote back.

As he looked at the sea Neil thought some more on The Grilse's bit about growing. The old guy wasn't all daft. No way. He searched around for a flat stone, of the right size, and sent it hopping through the rollers. Then he turned his back on the sea, walked up the beach and crossed the bank to The Grilse's house.

# Sunday Class

ELSPETH DAVIE 1968

This is a very short story about a single event – a clash of personalities, with a nice deadpan humour and a sense of developing tension about it. With the next story, 'Christian Endeavour' (page 93), it may remind us how important the church once was in Scottish society, and still is for many people.

This semicircle crouched around the teacher are dead on time with their answers. A well-drilled lot, they flick them back, one after the other, while the question is scarcely out of her mouth.

'Flowers.'

'Birds.'

'Good food.'

'Homes.'

'Friends.'

'And loved ones,' snaps the oldest girl jealously.

Now they all turn their heads to the boy at the end. They know there is nothing left for him except 'good books', 'good music' or perhaps 'sunshine' at a pinch. They wait for it. He stares stubbornly down towards the end of the room.

'Come on,' urges the woman, Miss MacRae, her eyes wavering from her lapel brooch to her wrist-watch. 'Some of the things God wants us to be grateful for?'

'Dinosaurs,' says the boy.

There is a pause while the woman shifts the fur about her neck. She looks warm. 'To be *grateful* for,' she warns.

'I know that. I said "dinosaurs".'

'I suppose you know what they are?'

'I know all about them. Always have.'

'And you know how to spell them?'

'It doesn't matter.'

'What did you say?'

'It doesn't matter.'

'Can you not think of anything else?'

'No. I'm thinking of them all the time.'

'*All* the time?' Her eyes narrow in suspicion.

'Well, someone had better think about them. They were around for millions of years. I'm grateful for them!'

There is reason to be grateful for the swinge and whack of the monstrous, scaly tails in this stifling hall. A quiver of relief runs through the others in the circle as they momentarily throw aside good books, homes and loved ones. They stare up towards the high sealed windows expectantly. In this East of Scotland town it is common enough to see things swirling in the air even at that height. On the stormiest days tufts of foam have sailed past and whole sodden newspapers flattened themselves out against the glass. Besides being a meeting-place for various classes during the week this hall is sometimes used for a dance, and on Sunday morning the sweaty dust of Saturday night still hangs in the air. On the platform stands a grand piano, swathed in green cloth. Along the wall behind it are various Bible pictures, maps and travel posters. There is also a chart showing a fair-haired young man balancing on the apex of a large isosceles triangle, and at graded levels beneath him a variety of animals stare wonderingly up, except for one or two leathery creatures near the bottom who continue to stare glumly at their own tails. The chap standing at the top looks glad to be where he is, but not surprised. He is not naked, as in some charts, but wears a casual sports shirt and flannel trousers. His pink, open palms are turned outwards to show that he has nothing to hide. His bare feet are also turned outwards.

Down both sides of the room, separated from one another by thin, wooden screens, are a dozen or so small circles seated around a man or a woman. From behind each screen comes a strange murmuring, discreet and low. It is like the murmurings of visitors in a hospital ward – sometimes placating, sometimes insistent or impatient, but always mesmerically soft. The boy who has dinosaurs on the brain keeps turning his head first to the stage and then to the door. Sometimes he tips his chair forward and cranes his neck as though to see around the neighbouring screens and to catch another murmur, perhaps to compare one murmur with another. Then he returns his attention to the woman in front of him, watching her mouth closely like a lip-reader or like somebody following a conversation in a foreign language. This irritates her more than anything else.

'I'm afraid that's not quite good enough,' she insists. 'I want something more.'

The rest of the class fix him with their eyes. They are afraid that now for the sake of peace he will hand her a good book or even a single perfect flower. But the boy broods. Now he is dredging through the deepest pits of the sea. Things not quite good enough for Miss MacRae spurt from fissures or prod the blackness with phosphorescent eye-stalks. Further up are creatures frilled, beaked and scalloped, some whip-thin, others round and smooth as bells. And far above in steaming tropical forests the ground crackles and glitters with ferocious insects. He has made his choice. He scratches his knee thoughtfully, then raises his hands and demonstrates something in the air.

'There's a sort of insect –' he ruminates. 'A giant fish-killing bug with claws that fold up under its head like a clasp-knife . . .'

'I am taking no notice of you,' Miss MacRae interrupts instantly, her eyes riveted on him. 'Everybody else can understand what I'm asking. Are you different from everyone else?' He is silent. They are all silent, studying Miss MacRae. In striking contrast to her lack of love for wildlife she is made up of scraps from various birds and beasts. She is sporting a tuft of bright coloured feathers, a couple of paws, a tail and a head and a carved bone or two. Her gloves are suede and she has a small purse-bag made of real pigskin lined with coarse hair. There is nothing artificial about her except the butterfly brooch in her lapel and the deep-set button eyes in the furry head that peers over her shoulder.

At the top of the room a handbell is struck loudly – signal that it is time to reassemble in the larger adjoining hall. Although most of the group snatch up magazines and bibles and stampede off as usual, a few – mostly the older girls – linger as though protectively about Miss MacRae. Today there are mixed feelings about her. Her dismissal of dinosaurs and her withdrawal from fish-killing bugs has shown her to be wildly outside and utterly alone. It seems there is no place to put her now. All the same some of them feel for her in their hearts, and the oldest girl strokes the face of the little fox consolingly.

But the boy remains uncompromisingly stern. He gives them all time to clear off to the next room and in the meantime he takes a closer look at the chart on the wall behind the platform. This look confirms something he has suspected for a long time. Now there is no doubt about it. Miss MacRae is the true, self-appointed mate of the chap standing on the sharp, topmost point of the isosceles triangle. Her place is up there beside him. But could the man bring himself to step aside one fraction of an inch to make room for her?

# Christian Endeavour

ALAN SPENCE 1977

Here is a semi-autobiographical tale which puts a spotlight on organised religion, Scottish-style – rather like the previous story. It pokes gentle fun at several of our old-fashioned notions: about rote learning by the book, and also about 'darkest Africa', which Scots once believed it was their mission not just to 'discover', but to convert to Christianity.

I had been a religious fanatic for only a few weeks.

'What is it the night then?' asked my father. 'The bandy hope?' I caught the mockery, but he meant no harm.

'Christian Endeavour,' I said, drying my face with a towel and stretching up to peer at myself in the cracked mirror above the sink. 'Band a Hope's on Thursday.'

The two halves of my face in the mirror didn't quite match because of the crack, were slightly out of alignment. It was an old shaving-mirror of my father's with an aluminium rim, hung squint from a nail in the window-frame.

'Ah thought Christian Endeavour was last night?'

'That was just the Juniors,' I said. 'Tonight's the Real one.'

'Are ye no too young?' said my father.

'The minister says ah can come.'

'Is that because ye were top in the bible exam?'

'Top equal,' I said. 'Ah don't know if that's why. He just said ah could come.'

'Ach well,' said my father, going back behind his newspaper. 'Keeps ye aff the streets.'

'Ah'll be the youngest there,' I said, proud of myself and wanting to share it.

'Mind yer heid in the door,' he said. 'It's that big ye'll get stuck.'

I pulled on my jacket and was ready to go.

'Seen ma bible?' I asked.

'Try lookin where ye left it,' he said.

I found it on the table with another book, *The Life of David Livingstone*, under the past week's heap of newspapers and comics. The book had been my prize in the bible exam.

The exam had been easy. Questions like *Who carried Christ's cross on the way to Calvary?* And from the Shorter Catechism, *Into what estate did the fall bring mankind?*

It was just a matter of remembering.

The label gummed in the book read FIRST PRIZE, with EQUAL penned in above BIBLE KNOWLEDGE, and then my name.

My father remembered reading the same book as a boy. He had been a sergeant in the Boys' Brigade, and the book had made him want to be a missionary himself.

'Great White Doctor an that,' he said. 'Off tae darkest Africa.'

But somehow he had drifted away from it all. 'Wound up in darkest Govan instead,' he said.

For the years he had been in the Boys' Brigade, he had been given a long-service badge. I still kept it in a drawer with a hoard of other badges I had gathered over the years. Most of them were cheap tin things, button badges: ABC Minors, Keep Britain Tidy. But the BB badge was special, heavier metal in the shape of an anchor. I had polished it with Brasso till it shone. There were two other treasures in the drawer: an army badge an uncle had given me, shaped like a flame, and a Rangers supporters badge, a silver shield with the lion rampant in red.

Christian Endeavour had a badge of its own. A dark blue circle with a gold rim, and CE in gold letters. The Sunday-school teachers at the Mission all wore it. I had been disappointed that there wasn't one for the Juniors. But now that I was moving up, I would be entitled to wear the badge. CE. In gold.

'Is ther gonnae be any other youngsters there the night?' asked my father.

'Jist Norman,' I said. Norman was the minister's son. He was twelve, a year older than me.

'Ye don't like him, do ye?'

'He's a big snotter,' I said. 'Thinks e's great.'

'Wis he top in the bible exam as well?'

'Top equal,' I said. My father laughed.

'That minister's quite a nice wee fella,' he said. 'That time he came up here, after yer mother died, we had quite a wee chat.'

'Aye, ye told me,' I said.

'Ah think he got a surprise. Wi me no goin tae church an that, he musta thought ah was a bitty a heathen. Expected tae find me aw bitter, crackin up y'know.'

'Aye, ah know.'

'But ah wisnae. Ah showed um ma long-service badge fae the BB. Even quoted scripture at him!'

'Aye.'

'"In my father's house there are many mansions," ah said. That's the text they read at the funeral.'

'Time ah was goin,' I said.

'He wanted me tae come tae church,' said my father. 'But ah cannae be bothered wi aw that. Anywey, you're goin enough for the two ae us these days, eh?'

'Aye. Cheerio, da.'

'See ye after, son.'

I took a last look at my reflection in the squinty mirror.

'Right,' I said.

I took the shortcut to the Mission, across the back courts. It was already dark, and in the light from the windows I could make out five or six boys in the distance. From their noise I could recognise them as my friends, and I hurried on, not really wanting them to see me. If they asked where I was going, they would only mock.

I hadn't been out with them this week, except for playing football after school. They thought I was soft in the head for going so much to the Mission. They couldn't understand. I felt a glow. It was good to feel good. It had come on stronger since my mother had died. The Mission was a refuge from the empty feeling of lack.

But part of me was always drawn back to my friends, to their rampaging and their madness.

I heard a midden-bin being overturned, a bottle being smashed, and the gang of boys scattered laughing through the backs as somebody shouted after them from a third-storey window. Head down, I hurried through a close and out into the street.

Now that I was almost at the Mission, I felt nervous and a little afraid. I had never been to an adult meeting before. I thought of the lapel-badge with the gold letters. CE. Perhaps I would even be given one tonight. Initiated.

(Douglas Corrance)

There was another badge I had seen the teachers wearing. It was green with a gold lamp, an oil lamp like Aladdin's. But maybe that was only for ministers and teachers.

*Give me oil in my lamp, keep me burning.*

*Give me oil in my lamp I pray,*

*Halleluja!*

The Mission hall was an old converted shop, the windows covered over with corrugated iron. A handwritten sign on the door read CHRISTIAN ENDEAVOUR. Tonight. 7.30. I stood for a moment, hesitating, outside. Then I pushed open the door and went in to the brightness and warmth.

I was early, and only a handful of people had arrived. They sat, talking, in a group near the front of the hall, and nobody seemed to have noticed me come in.

Norman was busy stacking hymn-books. Looking up, he saw me and nodded, then went out into the back room.

The minister saw me then and waved me over. There were two or three earnest conversations going on. The minister introduced me to a middle-aged African couple.

'These are our very special guests,' he said. 'Mr and Mrs Lutula.'

'How do you do,' we all said, and very formally shook hands. There was a momentary lull then the conversations picked up again. But I could feel the big black woman looking at me.

'And tell me,' she said, her voice deep like a man's, 'when did the Lord Jesus come into your heart?'

'Pardon?' I said, terrified.

'Ah said, when did the Lord Jesus come into your heart, child?'

That was what I thought she had said. And she wanted an answer. From me. I looked up at the broad face smiling at me, the dark eyes shining. I looked down at the floor. I could feel myself blush. What kind of question was that to ask? How was I supposed to answer it?

Why didn't she ask me something straightforward?

*Who carried Christ's cross on the way to Calvary?*

*Joseph of Aramathea.*

*Into what estate did the fall bring mankind?*

*The fall brought mankind into an estate of sin and misery.*

I sat, tense and rigid, on the hard wooden seat. Now my face was really hot and flushed. I cleared my throat. In a squeak of a voice I said, 'I don't know if . . .'

I looked at the floor.

She leaned over and patted my arm. 'Bless you, child,' she said, smiling, and turned to talk to her husband.

I stood up, still looking at the floor. I made my way, conscious of every step, clumsy and awkward, to the back of the hall and out into the street. I walked faster; I began to run, away from the Mission, along the street, through the close into the back court.

The night air cooled me. I stopped and leaned against a midden wall. I was in absolute misery, tortured by my own sense of foolishness. It wasn't just the question, it was what it had opened up; a realm where I knew nothing, could say nothing.

When did the Lord Jesus come into my heart? I could have said it was when my mother died. That would have sounded pious. But I didn't think it was true. I didn't know. That was it; I didn't know. If the Lord Jesus had come into my heart, I should know.

And how could I go back in now? It was all too much for me. I would tell the minister on Sunday I had felt hot and flushed, had gone outside for some air. That much was true. I would say I had felt sick and gone home.

The back court was quiet. There was no sound, except for the TV from this house or that. Bright lit windows in the dark tenement blocks. I walked on, slow, across the back, and as I passed another midden, I kicked over a bin, and ran.

Nearer home I slowed down again.

My father would ask why I was back so early.

# The Cure

LIZ LOCHHEAD 1995

In this contemporary teenage story, Gemma tells it like it is for a typical third-year girl in a Scottish secondary school, Staneyburn High. Her voice is honest, her speech is demotic Scots, and she has a nice line in irony. Like Newtongrange in 'The Face' (page 57), Staneyburn was a mining town, 'the pit shut, empty acres of industrial estate, the high street with half the shops boarded up . . . '

He goes: Aha, the very one I've been looking for.

I'm like, who me? Feeling this big beamer of a riddy creep up on my face. Trying to do a mind over matter over blushing.

He goes: Gemma, the very girl. Listen, Gems, you're gonny run the Intermediate Inter-House Mixed Relay, right?

I'm like that.

He says: Gie's a brekk, Gemma, don't look at us like that, you're white as a sheet, you'd think I'd asked you to do something scary or something. C'mon I've ticked your name alreadys, ask not what your House can do for you, ask what you can do for your House. Which is a measly hunner yards. Wan leg of a relay. A scoosh. Your Country Needs You.

And he points at us like yon Uncle Sam poster.

Och, away an –

Yes, Gemma?

Nuh. N.A.W. No way Ho-zay. I'm no daen it. That's what I should of says. All I get out, but, is: I canny . . . *please* don't . . . don't ask me.

But he got round us. Roy Speedie, House-Captain. Man of my dreams. The only person I've ever fancied.

He got round us. Dead easy. Would not take no for an answer. Pardon. I didn't catch that. You see I need you, Gemma, simple as that. You're running.

'Parently total shortage of females in the third year with initials between the letter S and the end of the alphabet, thus qualifying them as bonafidy born members of Dalhousie House, Staneyburn High. Seems there's just yon Robina Smiley (the fastest runner, swimming champion, centre-forward intermediate first eleven hockey team, Dux of the Year, Captain of the

Debating Team, leader of the God Squad, Duke of Edinburgh Award blah, blah, blah, etcetera) – well, *she's* running obviously. Then there's Julie Ann Taylor, who's just had the twins, Donna Scrimgeour, ME, Elaine Yuill, anorexia, and big gi-normous Sandra Veitch (glandular fat, no puppy). And me. Theory is I'll be best of a bad lot. Just cos I'm dead average-ish. Dead average-ish and dead dead-against sport of any kind.

Except – don't ask me why – late-night snooker on the telly. Mibbe it's because it reminds me of staying up late with my Dad when I was wee and getting a toty wee splash of lager into my lemonade and him going wheest, don't tell your mammy and winking, and then me thinking I was *it*, imagining my head was spinning because I'd drank a whole glass of shandy. He still watches the snooker with us when I go over to his during the holidays. We bet five ps. Other times at home I watch it myself because mum can't abide it.

Running, but. I'd run a mile from the very idea. Only Roy Speedie willny let us.

Janine Marshall and Margo Capaldi were smarming all over us the minute he'd left me. So. What did big Speedie want? Did he ask you out? I seen you blushing. Eh? What was he after? You gaun wi him to the Senior Disco? He really *likes* you, Gems. It's dead obvious intit, Margo? Oh aye, did you see the wey he smiled at her, eh, J?

Listen, here's my advice to you, and if you have any sense you'll take it. You fancy somebody, say nothing. Nothing. To nobody.

Look, I know how it is. You fall for somebody and it builds up. Inside. This feeling. An excitement. All the time. Dizzy and that. The usual. Say it's the first time, ever, that it's ever happened to you, you recognise it right away. As in the books, songs, movies. Yup, here you go. This is it. And the next thing, because you can't resist it at the time, you're blurting out to your best pal, just for the pure pleasure of saying his name out loud – which might feel, temporarily, like it's a release and a good idea – the whole true confession, listen, I-am-daft-about-so-and-so *mistake*. Which it is. Mibbe you can't help your feelings, but surely to god you can zip your mouth?

Wish I hud.

Instead I have to repeat to them what Roy Speedie has said. How it doesn't matter how badly I run in the race, the important thing is to try my best. For the sake of the team. For the sake of the House. That is all anybody can ask of me. That's all I can ask of myself. That's all Roy Speedie is asking.

I still think that's him working up to asking you out, goes Margo.

See what I mean about regretting that I opened my stupit trap? I might have had the pleasure of fantasising that myself. But hearing Margo coming out with it forces me to recognise it for the pathetic delusion it is. Margo doesn't believe it for a minute either. This is just the kind of crap your pals seem to be obliged to come out with. When they know your secret heart's desire.

The week leading up to the sports is a nightmare. I can't sleep. I feel sick. All I can think of is that unless I get run over by a bus or carted off to the hospital in an ambulance with a burst appendix, I will have to appear in front of the whole school in my gym shorts with my bare legs all measled wi granny's tartan with sitting reading too close to the gas fire all winter, and my Mum's aerobics trainers. Me, who am strictly a thick black tights and Doc Marten person. And, in front of the whole school, I will have to run. Despite the fact that, until I learned good foolproof skives to avoid such embarrassments, I regularly came in last in any heat of any first year athletic event. And Helen Paterson laughed at us, called us spiderlegs, and imitated me running by tying her knees together with a gym sash and then splay-footing along with sticky-out elbows waggling out of time till everybody knotted themselves.

My mother has no sympathy. She hopes I think nobody will have anything better to do with their time than look at me. Just do my best and that's all anybody can ask. She's never heard so much girning about nothing.

She's washed and pressed my gym kit.

The day of the sports is brilliant sunshine. It would be. Once the dreaded moment has arrived, but, I am strangely calm. Roy Speedie has already won the Senior 200 metres and the hurdles, and Dalhousie and Balfour Houses are running neck and neck in the Inter-House competition, so he and the Balfour House captains, a scrawny red-haired guy with white eyelashes called Billy Molyneux and a big blowsy girl with the very unfortunate name of Judy Peasgood, are pep-talking their teams for the Intermediate Inter-House Mixed Relay. Us. Balfour have just won the Junior Inter-House Relay and Dalhousie a very close second. Roy smiles at us. It's a great smile and I am not, myself, impressed by Janine Marshall's past comment that he doesny half know it. He smiles. Right at me. Similar melting effect as the day six months ago when I fell madly in love with him during Paul Jones at third year Christmas Dance. Senior House captains and prefects were also invited, although very few of the *female* prefects, funnily enough, bothered to turn up. Sixth year *guys* did, but. An obvious sickener for the acned bean-poles or waver-voiced smouts or specky swots with charisma bypasses that make up the boys in our year. So, when the music stopped, and there's Roy Speedie exactly half way between me and Judy Peasgood in a figured velvet frock that made her look like a settee or something, he just shrugs, smiles at me, takes my hands and whirls me away into the Gay Gordons, during which he asks my name – my name! – and holds me dead tight in the polka-ing bit so's he can get an extra birl in. When the music changes he winks at us, that smile again, and he's off. And I am in love. I recognised it right away. I keep it up for months. Nothing changes. Nothing particular seems to need to happen to keep it going. An occasional sighting, a walk past his house with Janine Marshall and an argument over whether that was him or his dad sitting there in front of the blue flickery light of the TV. Him walking past in the dinner school. This will do, apparently.

   And now the race. I have to do my best, that's all. Like I says, it's weird but I'm – suddenly – dead calm. An absence of butterflies. I walk to the third place. I'm on third. The team goes: Ronnie Urquhart, Robina Smiley, me, then Alasdair Speedie, Roy's wee brother.

   Nobody could fancy *him*. Ever.

   The race itself is weird. Time jerks from slow motion to speeded up then back again. On your marks, dead slow, get set, slower still, and *go*. Ronnie Urquhart is barrelling along with his head down and his arms going like pistons, but it's as if he's standing still, then, suddenly, he's round the bend and I've just got time to realise he's in the lead and the changeover to Robina Smiley is already made, clockwork, and she's charging towards me full tilt with a purple face and the mouth in it opens, Run! Run!, and she looks daggers, raging, honest if looks could kill, and my wee legs have finally started up but I'm still gawping at her and she's skelped the baton home into my mitt and the other third-person runners are starting up, one, two and three and they're after me getting the baton, God, Dalhousie must be in the lead, but, by the time I realise that, they're past me, and I'm doing my best, doing my best, giving it laldy, shoes skliffing off the gravel, it speeds up again, and jigging in front of me is the furious face of Roy's wee brother, c'mon, *c'mon*, and he's the last of the fourths still on his mark, he starts running, too quick, too quick, I can't catch him, he slows down again, slows down practically till a standstill, slows down slow enough till I can complete the baton pass, even then I nearly drop it, but, eventually, away he goes like the clappers into all the shouting and I'm finally doubled up, peching, with a stitch in my side as they cross the line, Balfour, Aitken, Crimmond and, last but not least, a poor fourth, Dalhousie. Bringing up the cow's tail.

Next thing Roy Speedie is by my side and he's screaming at me. You stupit, stupit bitch. We were winning, we were *first* and *you* – I stand back up straight. My stitch is gone. I seem to have my puff back. I feel . . . fantastic. This time it's me that smiles at him. I even consider winking. I shrug, but. I says: I tried my best. As you said yourself, nobody can ask more than that, Roy. And away I go to get changed.

Janine Marshall and Margo Capaldi seem to have difficulty believing it, but I am completely cured of love for Roy Speedie. They give me pitying glances when Roy Speedie and Robina Smiley – they seem to have taken up with each other – moon past hand in hand up the park at lunch time. They think I'm being brave when I say I'm not bothered. Margo says they deserve each other, Smiley Speedie and Speedy Smiley, but, quite honestly, it is a matter of no interest to me. As I fell in love with him in an instant so I fell out of love with him in an instant and now I am immune to his pointless good looks.

As, at the same time, I grew out of the Glory of The School, Do Your Best, Healthy Competition, Pillar of the British Empire, Second Hand Imitation Public School carry-on. I mean, you look at Staneyburn, the pit shut, empty acres of industrial estate, the high street with half the shops boarded up (bar Poundstretcher), twenty folk trying to sell you the *Big Issue* to wan flogging *Militant*; and our school, which, despite its golden past as a Senior Secondary, is just a local comprehensive pure and simple, tries to uphold the idea that the most important thing is winning the House Shield and being elected by a jury of your peers to high office and the wearing of the Prefects' Braid. And is there honey still for tea? Get real.

I became, the instant I fell out of love with Roy Speedie, one of the apathetic ones the headmaster castigates in school assembly. This thought makes me quite cheery. Inside myself I have a laboratory of interesting emotions. I am a woman of experience. I have fallen in love. I have fallen out of love. Someday, mibbe when they grow up a bit, Janine Marshall and Margo Capaldi might understand.

Two boys at the old confectioner's, Gorbals, Glasgow (Oscar Marzaroli)

# Away in Airdrie

JAMES KELMAN 1983

This story reminds us that many Scots are football fanatics who will, like Danny, 'go anywhere for a game'. It also reminds us that most young people have to cope, somewhere along the line, with an 'unreliable' adult like Uncle Archie.

Airdrie is not far from Glasgow, and its football team plays at Broomfield Park, about whose small-town delights city-boy Danny is understandably sniffy. The colours of Glasgow Rangers, one of Scotland's top teams, are blue, red and white. Airdrie sports a mere blue and white.

During the early hours of the morning the boy was awakened by wheezing, spluttering noises and the smell of a cigarette burning. The blankets hoisted up and the body rolled under, knocking him over onto his brother. And the feet were freezing, an icy draught seemed to come from them. Each time he woke from then on he could either smell the cigarette or see the sulphur head of the match flaring in the dark. When he opened his eyes for the final time the man was sitting up in bed and coughing out: Morning Danny boy, how's it going?

I knew it was you.

Aye, my feet I suppose. Run through and get me a drink of water son will you.

Uncle Archie could make people laugh at breakfast, even Danny's father – but still he had to go to work. He said, If you'd told me you were coming I could've made arrangements.

Ach, I was wanting to surprise yous all. Uncle Archie grinned: You'll be coming to the match afterwards though eh?

The father looked at him.

The boys're through at Airdrie the day.

Aw aye, aye. The father nodded, then he shrugged. If you'd told me earlier Archie – by the time I'm finished work and that . . .

Uncle Archie was smiling: Come on, long time since we went to a match the gether. And you're rare and handy for a train here as well.

Aye I know that but eh; the father hesitated. He glanced at the other faces round the table. He said, Naw Archie. I'll have to be going to my work and that, the gaffer asked me in specially. And I dont like knocking him back, you know how it is.

Ach, come on –

Honest, and by the time I finish it'll be too late. Take the boys but. Danny – Danny'll go anywhere for a game.

Uncle Archie nodded for a moment. How about it lads?

Not me, replied Danny's brother. I've got to go up the town.

Well then . . . Uncle Archie paused and smiled: Me and you Danny boy, eh!

Aye Uncle Archie. Smashing.

Here! – I thought you played the game yourself on Saturdays?

No, the father said, I mean aye – but it's just the mornings he plays, eh Danny?

Aye. Aw that'll be great Uncle Archie. I've never been to Broomfield.

It's no a bad wee park.

Danny noticed his mother was looking across the table at his father while she rose to tidy away the breakfast stuff. He got up and went to collect his football gear from the room. The father also got up, he pulled on his working coat and picked his parcel of sandwiches from the top of the sideboard. When the mother returned from the kitchen he kissed her on the cheek and said he would be home about half past two, and added: See you when you get back Archie. Hope the game goes the right way.

No fear of that! We'll probably take five off them. Uncle Archie grinned, You'll be kicking yourself for no coming – best team we've had in years.

Ach well, Danny'll tell me all about it. Okay then . . . he turned to leave. Cheerio everybody.

The outside door closed. Uncle Archie remained by himself at the table. After a moment the mother brought him an ashtray and lifted the saucer he had been using in its stead. He said, Sorry Betty.

You're smoking too heavy.

I know. I'm trying to . . . He stopped; Danny had come in carrying a tin of black polish and a brush, his football-boots beneath his arm. As he laid the things in front of the fireplace he asked: You seen my jersey mum?

It's where it should be.

The bottom drawer?

She looked at him. He had sat down on the carpet and was taking the lid off the tin of black polish. She waited until he placed an old newspaper under the things, before leaving the room.

Hey Danny, called the Uncle. You needing any supporters this morning?

Supporters?

Aye, I'm a hell of a good shouter you know. Eh, wanting me along?

Well . . .

What's up? Uncle Archie grinned.

Glancing up from the book he was reading Danny's brother snorted; He doesnt play any good when people's watching.

Rubbish, cried Danny, it's not that at all. It's just that – the car Uncle Archie, see we go in the teacher's car and there's hardly any space.

With eleven players and the driver! Uncle Archie laughed: I'm no surprised.

But I'll be back in plenty of time for the match, he said as he began brushing the first boot.

Aye well you better because I'll be off my mark at half twelve pronto. Mind now.

Aye.

It's yes, said the mother while coming into the room, she was carrying two cups of fresh tea for herself and Uncle Archie.

Danny was a bit embarrassed, walking with his uncle along the road, and over the big hill leading out from the housing scheme, down towards the railway station in Old Drumchapel. But he met nobody. And there was nothing wrong with the scarf his uncle was wearing, it just looked strange at first, the blue and white, really different from the Rangers' blue. But supporters of a team were entitled to wear its colours. It was better once the train had stopped at Queen Street Station. Danny was surprised to see so many of them all getting on, and hearing their accents. In Airdrie Uncle Archie became surrounded by a big group of them, all laughing and joking. They were passing round a bottle and opening cans of beer.

Hey Danny boy come here a minute! Uncle Archie reached out to grip him by the shoulder, taking him into the middle of the group. See this yin, he was saying: he'll be playing for Rangers in next to no time . . . The men stared down at him. Aye, went on his uncle, scored two for the school this morning. Man of the Match.

That a fact son? called a man.

Danny reddened.

You're joking! cried Uncle Archie. Bloody ref chalked another three off him for offside! Eh Danny?

Danny was trying to free himself from the grip, to get out of the group.

Another man was chuckling: Ah well son you can forget all about the Rangers this afternoon.

Aye you'll be seeing a *team* the day, grunted an old man who was wearing a bunnet with blue and white checks.

Being in Broomfield Park reminded him of the few occasions he had been inside Hampden watching the Scottish Schoolboys. Hollow kind of air. People standing miles away could be heard talking to each other, the same with the actual players, you could hear them grunting and calling out names. There was a wee box of a Stand that looked like it was balancing on stilts.

The halftime score was one goal apiece. Uncle Archie brought him a bovril and a hot pie soaked in the watery brown sauce. A rare game son eh? he said.

Aye, and the best view I've ever had too.

Eat your pie.

The match had ended in a two all draw. As they left the terracing he tagged along behind the group Uncle Archie was walking in. He hung about gazing into shop windows when the game was being discussed, not too far from the station. His uncle was very much involved in the chat and after a time he came to where Danny stood. Listen, he said, pointing across and along the road. See that cafe son? Eh, that cafe down there? Here, half a quid for you – away and buy yourself a drink of ginger and a bar of chocolate or something.

Danny nodded.

And I'll come and get you in a minute.

He took the money. I'm just nipping in for a pint with the lads . . .

Have I to spend it all?

The lot. Uncle Archie grinned.

I'll get chips then, said Danny, but I'll go straight into the cafe and get a cup of tea after, okay?

Fair enough Danny boy fair enough. And I'll come and get you in fifteen minutes pronto. Mind and wait till I come now.

Danny nodded.

He was sitting with an empty cup for ages and the waitress was looking at him. She hovered about at his table till finally she snatched the cup out of his hands. So far he had spent twenty-five pence and he was spending no more. The remaining money was for school through the week. Out from the cafe he crossed the road, along to the pub. Whenever the door opened he peered inside. Soon he could spot his uncle, sitting at a long table, surrounded by a lot of men from the match. But it was impossible to catch his attention, and each time he tried to keep the door open a man seated just inside was kicking it shut.

He wandered along to the station, and back again, continuing on in the opposite direction; he was careful to look round every so often. Then in the doorway of the close next to the pub he lowered himself to sit on his heels. But when the next man was entering the pub Danny was onto his feet and in behind him, keeping to the rear of the man's flapping coat tails.

You ready yet Uncle Archie?

Christ Almighty look who's here.

The woman's closing the cafe.

Uncle Archie had turned to the man sitting beside him: It's the brother's boy.

Aw, the man nodded.

What's up son?

It's shut, the cafe.

Just a tick, replied Uncle Archie. He lifted the small tumbler to his lips, indicated the pint glass of beer in front of him on the table. Soon as I finish that we'll be away son. Okay? I'll be out in a minute.

The foot had stretched out and booted the door shut behind him. He lowered himself onto his heels again. He was gazing at an empty cigarette packet, it was being turned in abrupt movements by the draught coming in the close. He wished he could get a pair of wide trousers. The mother and father were against them. He was lucky to get wearing long trousers at all. The father was having to wear short trousers and he was in his last year at school, just about ready to start serving his time at the trade. Boys nowadays were going to regret it for the rest of their days because they were being forced into long trousers before they needed to. Wide trousers. He wasnt bothered if he couldnt get the ones with the pockets down the sideseams, the ordinary ones would do.

The door of the pub swung open as a man came out and passed by the close. Danny was at the door. A hot draught of blue air and the smells of the drink, the whirr of the voices, reds and whites and blues and whites all laughing and swearing and chapping at dominoes.

He walked to the chip shop.

Ten number tens and a book of matches Mrs, for my da.

The woman gave him the cigarettes. When she gave his change he counted it slowly, he said: Much are your chips?

Same as last time.

Will you give us a milky-way, he asked.

He ate half of the chocolate and covered the rest with the wrapping, stuck it into his pocket. He smoked a cigarette; he got to his feet when he had tossed it away down the close.

Edging the door ajar he could see Uncle Archie still at the table. The beer was the same size as the last time. The small tumbler was going back to his lips. Danny sidled his way into the pub, but once inside he went quickly to the long table. He was holding the torn-in-half tickets for the return journey home, clenched in his right hand. He barged a way in between two men and put one of the tickets down on the table quite near to the beer glass.

I'm away now Uncle Archie.

What's up Danny boy?

Nothing. I'm just away home . . . He turned to go then said loudly: But I'll no tell my mother.

He pushed out through the men. He had to get out, Uncle Archie called after him but on he strode sidestepping his way beyond the crowded bar area.

Twenty minutes before the train would leave. In the waiting room he sat by the door and watched for any sign of his uncle. It was quite quiet in the station, considering there had been a game during the afternoon. He found an empty section in a compartment of the train, closed the door and all of the windows, and opened the cigarette packet. The automatic doors shut. He stared back the way until the train had entered a bend in the track then stretched out, reaching his feet over onto the seat opposite. He closed his eyes. But had to open them immediately. He sat up straight, he dropped the cigarette on the floor and then lifted it up and opened the window to throw it out; he shut the window and sat down, resting his head on the back of the seat, he gazed at the floor. The train crashed on beneath the first bridge.

The black horse, from an old Celtic fairy tale. According to tradition, people who dared to mount a kelpie or waterhorse never dismounted, but were carried off to the bottom of the sea or the loch.

# The Man in the Boat

BETSY WHYTE 1981

> This is a recording of an oral folk tale, as told by Betsy Whyte to students
> at the School of Scottish Studies, in Edinburgh University, in 1981. So
> it is from Scotland's rich oral tradition of folk tales and fairy tales,
> stretching back *via* Robert Louis Stevenson's 'Tod Lapraik' and Robert
> Burns's 'Tam o Shanter' to the old Border ballads.
>
> The idea that everyone should be able to tell a story to help pass an
> idle hour may seem strange in the age of instant canned entertainment,
> but it is a very old one and crops up in many world literatures.

This story is aboot a laird awa in the Heilands . . . and he had the Black Art
. . . but every year he used to gie a big ceilidh for aa the workers on his
estate, an aa the fairm folk an aa the fairm hands, an he used tae had this
ceilidh in a big barn. There wis a fire in this barn, an they'd put on a big pot
of sowens. (Ye ken whit sowens are? No? Well Scotland, it's always been a
very poor country, and no that very long ago, jist aboot a hundred years
ago, they used to soak . . . the husks o the grain . . . until they were soor,
and then they strained it an boiled up the liquid an this made a sort of
porridge, and a lot o them had to exist on that.) So this big pot o sowens
wis boilin away anywey, and everybody wis doin their thing: ye hed tae

> *Tell a story,*
> *Sing a sang,*
> *Show yir bum*
> *Or oot ye gang!*

They hed other things as well as singin an tellin stories an that: they hed
sort of games, they'd games of strength an guesses an that sort o thing, and
one o the things wis to see who could tell the biggest lie. So everybody wis
gaun their roond and gaun their roond, but every time it came tae this
cattleman he would ay say, 'Ye ken fine I cannae dae nothing, ye shouldnae
ask me! Ye ken I cannae dae it.'

So this laird says, 'Look, ye can surely tell a lie.'

He says, 'No, A cannae.' Sandy wis a bit simple, ye ken, and he wisnae
very good at nothin but lookin efter the coos.

So the laird says, 'Sandy, look, try an tell a story, or tell us a lie o some kind.'

He says, 'A cannae, I dinnae ken how tae.'

'Well,' the laird says, 'if ye dinnae ken how tae ye're no gaunnae be here. Awa ye go an mak yirsel useful some other place.'

He says, 'What am I gaunnae dae?'

He says, 'I'll tell ye what tae dae. Awa ye go doon tae the water an clean my boat, because A'll be usin it shortly.' He says, 'Awa ye go.' So Sandy's away, tramp, tramp, tramp, doon through the gutters tae this river, this big river. And he scraped aa the moss an dirt aff the boat, scrapin it oot, and there wis a baler lyin in the boat an he wis balin oot the water an balin oot the water, an he steps inside the boat so that he could finish balin it oot, ye see?

But didn't this boat take off wi him, an there's no wey he could stop it! An before he could get time to think, even, they're away in the middle o the water, and he couldnae swim. So he says, 'Ach, A'll jist sit an let it go wherever it wants tae go.' So he jist sat like this lookin up at the birds an things.

But he glanced doon again, and there he saw the loveliest wee green satin slippers; pure silk stockins; taffeta dress – he says, 'Whit's this? Whit's this?' an he felt his sel ower – oh! pappies an everything! 'Oh!' he says. 'Whit's happenin?' Curls an everything. As he looked . . . ower the side o the boat, an there wis the bonniest lassie that ye ever saw lookin back at him. 'What's happened?' he says, 'What's happened? (higher voice) *What's happened?*' His voice changed all of a sudden. Oh! So he says, 'Oh, my God!' – he was so stunned he jist sat there, and this boat, it got tae the other side, an he felt . . . it was the boat scrapin the bottom that brought him back tae himsel, ye see – but he was a she now!

So she stands up in this lovely green claes, an she looked – she wondered how she wis gaunnae get oot o the boat withoot makin a mess o her shoes an everything. Now there wis a young man walkin alang the bank o the river, and when he looked doon an sa this young lassie in this boat, 'course he would run doon an help her oot. So he ran doon and he cairried her oot o the boat till he got her on dry land, an he says, 'Where are ye goin?'

'I don't know,' she says. 'I don't really know where I'm goin.'

He says, 'Well, where did ye come from?'

'Oh, I came from the other side o the water.'

'Are ye goin tae anybody?'

'I don't know.'

He says, 'Lassie, I think you must have fell an bumped yir heid. I think you've lost yir memory wi aa this "Don't knows, don't knows".'

She says, 'Well, mebbe something like that happened.' She says, 'I jist don't know where A'm goin here. Ye see, A know where A'm goin when A'm at the other side o the water, but A don't know where A'm goin here.'

'Well,' he says, 'A think A'll take ye home tae ma mother, an get her tae look after ye, see if ye get yir memory back.' So he took her home tae his mother, and she helped his mother in the hoose an did this an that. But in time he got aafae fond o her, in fact he fell in love wi her, and the two o them got married. And within a couple o year they had two o the bonniest wee bairns ye ever saw, a wee toddler and one in the pram.

So one day, when they were oot walkin wi the bairns, an he was pushin his pram, quite proud o this wee laddie he got, ye see . . . she says, 'Ye know, I think we'll go a walk down the river today.' She says, 'A haven't been back down that way since the day A came here.'

He says, 'Well, that's a good idea.' He says, 'It might bring back yir memory,' he says, 'if nothing else has all this time.'

She says, 'That's right.' So away they go down the riverside, and, sure enough, the wee boat wis still sittin there. 'Aw,' she says, 'look at it! It's all covered wi moss an lichen an aa kinds o dirt: A must go doon an clean it.'

So she ran doon the bank: she says, 'You keep the bairns here an A'll run doon the bank an clean it.' Down she goes, an she's scrapin away at it, an the baler wis still lyin in it, an she startit to bale oot the water. And in the end she stepped intae the boat to bale oot the last, an ye can guess whit happen't! This boat's away wi her again, and it kept goin an kept goin, and the fella – there wis no wey he could stop it, it went so fast, an he couldnae swim efter it, so he jist had to stand there and let it go.

Now half way across the water, when she lookit doon, there wis the auld tackety boots, auld moleskin troosers covered wi coo shairn, whiskers an baird an . . . this auld sleeved waistcoat, an he looked ower intae the water an there wis this cattleman . . . wi his teeth all broon wi tobacco juice an everything. 'Oh my God!' He started to roar an greet, an howl an greet, 'Oh, ma man an ma bairns! Ma man an ma bairns! Ma man an ma bairns . . .' and he jist sat like this and the tears trippin him, until the boat scraped the other side: an the boat took him right back tae where it had started aff.

Then Sandy jumpit oot the boat, an he ran and ran greetin and sobbin an sobbin an greetin. An when he ran up tae the fairm, this ceilidh's still gaun on, see? an the pot o sowens is still on the fire! An he cam in howlin an greetin an sobbin, an the laird says tae him, 'Whit's adae wi ye, Sandy?'

'Oh, dinnae speak tae me, dinnae speak tae me,' he says. 'Wheesht, leave me alane – wid ye leave me alane? Ma man an ma bairns! Ma man an ma bairns!'

'Man an bairns?' the laird says. 'Whit are ye speakin aboot?'

'Oh, would you wheesht?' he says.

'Sandy, come in here. Come on an sit doon beside . . . me here an tell us aa aboot it!' So Sandy came in an he sat doon beside the laird, an between sobbin an greetin he tells them aa aboot his man an his bairns.

An the laird says, 'Well, Sandy, that's the biggest lee we've heard the nicht, so you've won the golden guinea!'

That's the end o that one. Ye see the laird had pit a glamourie ower him, so that he thought aa this had happen't tae him, but actually he'd only been awa aboot twenty minutes.

# The Man in the Lochan

EONA MACNICOL 1969

Like 'The Man in the Boat' (page 113), here is a story which seems to come from the supernatural folk tradition which has always been popular in Scotland. But does it?

Note at the start of the story that it is set in a carefully depicted Highland landscape, in Glen Urquhart, beside Loch Ness (and we all know what lives there). That kind of realistic detail is often an effective 'trick' of the supernatural writer.

My mother's girlhood home was a croft above Clachanree proper, over its skyline, in the middle of the moor. A solitary place; I doubt if there were any other houses within view. Only the smoke from the houses of Tallurach and perhaps the schoolhouse behind the Planting gave hint of neighbours at all. We looked on to a sheer hill face called the Leitir which overshadowed Loch Laide, famous for its trout and for the waterfowl that lived secretly among its reeds.

A solitary place. When once I spent a whole summer there I found it too solitary. When I grew tired of watching women's ploys about the house I had to go about with my grandfather, tending his fields or rounding up his sheep. It must have been on an expedition with him that I discovered behind the Leitir a habitation I had never known about before.

It was a tiny croft, an islet of cultivation in the middle of the heather. There were only three fields, one of hay, one of turnips, one of potatoes, with a little grassland heavily encroached upon by tufts of bulrushes, even starred here and there by bog-cotton flowers. But in my eyes the smallness was its charm. On the greensward round the little house some half-dozen hens daintily strutted. A cow and her calf munched near by, and a pony lay taking his ease in shelter of the single tutelary rowan tree. An old woman could be seen busy on one of the fields, singling turnips.

I do not think it was the custom in Clachanree for women to work much in the fields. True, they would help out at harvest or lambing time. Here was a woman who every time I passed that way with my grandfather was at man's work. I admired her greatly. She was only of average height, but

*Cottages, Corrie,* drawing by Joan Eardley, 1947

stalwart and strong. How nonchalantly would she swing a hammer down upon a post in her fence; how confidently catch and harness her pony; with what careless ease cut rushes for his bed. Her clothes were the dark long-sleeved blouse and the full skirt that all elderly women wore, but she had man's boots, stout hob-nailed affairs; and I thought her worthy of them.

I persuaded my grandfather one day to pass near enough the house to hail her. 'Well, well then, Oonagh, and how are you the day?' She dropped her hoe and came silent though smiling to meet us. She wore her hair, of a silvery gold colour, in a pile on the top of her head, as the fashion then was or had been. Her face was brown with the sun, the corners of her eyes wrinkled from squinting against it.

I got into the habit of giving my grandfather the slip and spending with Oonagh the time I was out under his care. I made advances to her, and she accepted my presence in her silent way. I had the privilege of assisting her out of doors; gathering her cut hay, or making a mixture of milk and meal for her calf. Soon I was permitted entry into her house. Its thatch was adorned by a plume of heather sprouting all joco from it. Inside it consisted of only one room – well, one and a half, for the boxbed was virtually a room in itself. Everything was as spic-and-span as if Oonagh expected company. The coverlet of patchwork though frayed was immaculately clean; the table was covered in a shiny, bright-coloured stuff called, I think, baize; the bowls and jugs upon the dresser made as brave a display, proportionately to the size of the dwelling, as did ours in the croft house of Druim. Even the rag rug before the hearth was clean – clean, I began to realise, because few feet trod on it. There was no plant on the window sill; instead there was a brown jam-jar of pink-spotted flowers with a heavy clinging scent which vied with the usual smell of damp and peatreek. I had not at that time seen orchids. Oonagh in few words explained to me that she found them away out on the moor, among the peat bogs. I resolved I would go myself and find some.

Only one thing seemed to me to spoil the charm of the little dwelling; for joined on to the one room, like an envious poor neighbour, was the other half of the original house, now in a ruinous state. When I asked Oonagh why she did not have the old walls carried away she laughed, colour rose in her face, and she said, in a rare burst of talk, 'Who knows, *m'eudail*, but some day there will be need of them?'

She was not only silent, but strange. Yet I found it pleasanter to be with her than in jollier homes where there was always the likelihood of tedious talk, likening one's face to this and that past member of the family. Oonagh did not tease me with talk at all. In friendly silence we worked together, or rested; for sometimes she would fetch me out a glass of milk and a hunk of oatcake, and would herself sit down, her legs in the dark skirt spread comfortably upon the grass. She might hum to herself, or sing, more often in Gaelic but sometimes in English learnt at school. One song was a ballad of great length the chorus of which I picked up:

> 'I wish I were,
>     But I wish in vain,
> I wish I were
>     A young lass again.
> But such a thing
>     Can never be
> Till an Aipple grows
>     On an Oarange tree.'

Other times she might bring out of her pocket a clay pipe, and light up and puff away as good as any man.

One day as I was making my way to Oonagh's I heard a creaking sound, as of wheels on a rough rocky road. It was Oonagh going up on the high moor to turn her peats. And the sound was like a fairy pipe to me. I longed to be up on the heights in the sea of heather. Maybe too I should find those exotic pink-spotted flowers. The cart had got a start on me, yet it was going slowly, the pony straining with the effort of pulling, Oonagh walking beside.

I took short cuts and made up on them. I called a greeting to Oonagh, who said nothing in reply but looked as if she were not averse to my presence. She was smoking her clay pipe, curls of grey smoke floating backward in the wind. We plodded uphill behind the pony, who kept on nodding his head, poor thing, as if endorsing our unspoken complaints about the steepness of our way. At last we gained the peat moor, and Oonagh got busy turning, puffing the while at her pipe, saying nothing.

I for my part was content; there was so much to see. Among the heather grew blaeberry bushes with their vivid green, and staghorn moss paved that hidden world which is inhabited by lizards and beetles. But I found no flowers. And after a while I came back to Oonagh where she was turning the wet sides of peat to the wind. The wind had teased out strands of her grey-gold hair, and she squinted against sun and smoke. An old woman, with little power to amuse. I began to think it was time we were getting home.

But Oonagh took her pipe out of her mouth and said, 'Sheep.' I gathered she was uneasy about their whereabouts and wanted to scan the hill grazing ground. We left the pony patiently switching from his flanks the flies that settled whenever the wind dropped. We went round a hillock. I gasped with delight.

There lay a lochan, sleek, still, its dark surface sprinkled round the rim with water lilies of purest white. As fast as I could through the deep heather I made my way to it, and threw myself down on my stomach, stretching out a greedy hand for the nearest of the exquisite flowers. I secured one, but it had a long rubbery stem which seemed endless as it came up out of the water. I broke off the flower head. But so far from feeling satisfied, I felt greedier than ever and reached out farther for another flower. It was beyond my reach. I called to Oonagh, who had come back but made no effort to assist me, begging her to see if her longer arm could secure it.

I remember she came slowly, as if weighted down by her long heavy skirt and heavy boots, then got down awkwardly beside me. The wind had dropped for the moment. It was so still that reflections appeared in the water as if in a glass; the dark shape of the hillock; the clouds patterning the blue of the sky; a wild duck flying up to meet its counterpart flying down. Close to the brink our two reflections appeared. Then a small breeze came, and wrinkled the surface. The images were gone. Oonagh put out her arm. Her brown fingers closed below a flower and she pulled at it, dragging the stem like a discovered thing up and out. Another and another she procured, some six or seven, cheerful and humming, her pipe laid down by her side.

I was about to say I had enough and restrain Oonagh from further effort, when I found there was no need. The wind had dropped once more. The surface of the lochan was smooth, with images appearing on it again. Now Oonagh was bending so low her face almost met the water, shading her eyes with a hand spread on either side.

'What is it, Oonagh?' I asked. 'What are you looking at? Are there fish?'

'Aye are there fish!' She turned her head over her shoulder to address me. Her wrinkled sunburnt face wore a radiant smile. 'Put you your head down low and keep looking, *m'eudail*, and you will be seeing them. Grey like silver they are, leaping this way and that. Then suddenly they will leave the water and fly through the air.'

'How can fish leave the water? They would die.'

She said 'Tst!' impatiently, and turned from me to gaze into the water again. I felt I was missing something and followed her example, bending down so low I smelt the heavy smell of water thick with weeds.

She was staring in, rapt, like a clairvoyant.

'What are you seeing now?' I pestered her.

She pointed. 'See, see! See the palm trees moving.' I could see the stems of the water lilies swaying to some little depth, the currents moving them.

'That's not – ' Something stopped the words on my tongue, the realisation of the absurdity of it: how could palm trees grow in this cold windy place? I looked closely at Oonagh to see if she were joking at my expense. I took it upon myself to say, 'See will you fall in!'

She cried sharply, *'Bith sochd!'* – Be quiet! Her pointing finger moved like a magician's over the still water. 'Look now, what bonnie! A lily pool, it is lined with white stone, and a fountain in the middle of it, and the fishes are golden – look at them jinking this way and that way between the flowers. White the flowers are, as sheets laid – ' If I had a question I could not ask it, for something froze the words upon my lips. 'See yon! There it is, the house itself. It's coming. Look at that now!' She turned her face towards me, smiling but with eyes unfocused, then turned to the water again. Her voice was so low it was all I could do to catch what she said.

What house? What house? I had heard – who has not? – of houses, villages, overwhelmed by water, but away up here on the moor who had at any time built houses ? And how could a little lochan cover them?

She put a hand on my back and pressed me down. 'Here, look down here. Can you not see the house? It's down there, deep, deep in. The white pillars and the steps and the roof with a shine on it. That's the stars, *m'eudail*, bonnie stars they have there.'

I would have liked to ask her to let us leave the lochan and be going home. Indeed I rose up on my knees, but she was talking still, chuckling to herself. 'Aye there's them! There's the dark men, it's coming this time, the dark men with the bright clothes on them.'

I felt a longing for home keener than my past longing for water lilies. The game, if game it was, was over for me. I should never be able to see more in the lochan than lily stems and the reflections of hill and cloud and our own faces. There clear in the water I saw Oonagh's face, and was startled out of my senses; for the face in the water was young, the curve of cheek and chin like a girl's. I looked in astonishment from the reflected to the real face and found it was indeed bright, youthful, transfigured with joy.

She was chanting to herself in an ecstasy, 'When it is quiet he will come, himself will come. Out from between the pillars of his house, into my arms.' Her ecstasy melted into tears, and she cried with both smiles and tears, *'Tha m'ulaidh ort! Tha m'ulaidh!'* – I love you! I love you!

I cried out to her in fear, 'Oonagh!' And just as I spoke, a stiff breeze came. It ruffled the water from middle to brink. The still mirror was gone.

She jumped up and looked round at me in intense anger. Her face, old and brown, menaced me. Then, as if passing through a double enchantment, she was quiet and serene again, familiar, friendly, my companion of the summer.

She said, sighing, 'Aye aye, just so. It is always the way. He willna stay for long. There's aye a something. But when it is his time, he will come and stay.' She looked down at her knees where the damp peaty earth had stained her dark skirt, and stooped and picked up her clay pipe and stuck it between her lips. She took it out once to ask me, 'What were we doing at the lochan?' But I was now the silent one. I left my lilies behind, and walked with dragging steps after the cart and pony.

I was late home that evening. My mother was helping my grandmother at her churning. She called to me. Where had I been? My grandfather had come home without me.

I said I had been talking to Oonagh. Then, in a sudden longing to be reassured, I told the whole of it; about the lochan and how she had stared down into its depths and spoken of things she could see. My mother cried out, then stopped short with a hand at her mouth. It was left to my grandmother to speak. 'You must not go far from the place with Oonagh. It is not safe. Your grandfather should have warned you.'

'Why?' I cried, angry at the hint of blame.

My mother had regained control over herself. 'There is nothing against her, Ellen. Nothing at all. She is a good woman. For all they do not like her in their houses at such times as churning, she is respected. She has never done harm to a living. She is even mindful of the means of grace' – by which she meant she was a churchgoer – 'All the same, you will do well to keep away from her when she goes near water.' She made a signal to my grandmother.

But my grandmother did not see it or did not heed. 'She fell in love with the lochan itself, they say.' She paused maddeningly, took off the wooden lid and pulled the plunger up, a weird mass of horsehair and cream, and tested for butter forming. 'Some say the *eachd uisge* has put a spell upon her.'

My mother cried out along with me in remonstrance. My grandmother at last saw what was required of her and said nothing more, but began to churn mightily, singing a Psalm to swallow up any inauspicious influence and make the butter come firm and sweet.

My mother came to me when I was in bed. 'About the *eachd uisge*; you must not be afraid. There is no such thing. Your father, at any rate, would not approve of it. And about her being in love with the lochan; that is all nonsense, for she had a human lover. That is to say, there was a man she loved.' Her blue eyes grew thoughtful. The story hid within them. I lay still in my bed, listening with an eagerness near to apprehension. Yet it was like a story told already, I needed only the details.

It was some childish disappointment – my mother thought that Oonagh's new dress, such a rare possession, had been usurped by a sister – which made her run away over the moors to the lochan to hide her tears there. By its brink she should have been alone, but she began to hear the small clatter of oars in rowlocks. Curiosity drew her. It was not Jock from Corrie, nor Lachlan from Reneudin: it was a stranger. He was as startled as she was – and no wonder! – to see as if growing out of the moor this fair young girl. When he saw that she was weeping, however, he pulled in to the shore. 'Why are you weeping?' He asked it in Gaelic, that tender language; and in the same tongue she answered him, 'For nothing at all.' For suddenly it seemed as nothing. When he put a kindly hand to her head, straightening the snood ribbon, a feeling she had never known swept all through her, swept over him too.

Often after that, so ran my mother's whispered tale in the darkening room, they met at the lochan. He had come for a holiday to Glen Urquhart, for the fishing. He would take his boat out and sit with dipped oars, while she knelt at the boat's rim trying to see his image in the water, too shy still to look directly at him. Later they would lie by the brink. What passed between them my mother did not say, nor would I have known.

Summer was almost over when he told her what surely she must have known all the time. He was going away, not to the town, not even to Aberdeen or to Glasgow; over the unimaginable seas to a foreign land.

Seeing her face, he avowed, 'I will not forget you. One day when I have got rich I will come back and we will be always together.' She saw his image there in the water as he said it; saw it plainly in the still water, for all time, for ever. Then a breeze came and it was gone.

I could picture Oonagh as winter set in, snow on the far mountains, a bitter wind searing the nearer hills. In the cold of the morning she would crouch at the hearth, relighting the fire, clinging to her dreams, unwilling to leave them for the long vacuous day. But she was not forgotten, my mother said. Letters, a great novelty, came from foreign parts. Many people would have liked to examine them, but she would snatch them and run away with them over the moor to the lochan. It was in her light step and her singing that the contents of the letters could be guessed at. But sometimes she talked of the marvels of life abroad. So fantastic it seemed that people laughed as if at a jest.

Then after a while – did I not know? – the letters stopped coming. Months went by, seasons went by, and years. I pictured them in the mutations of the rowan tree: its young leaves; its pale blossom; its berries going from green to orange to red; then the tree bare again. But the reality was toil, long toil, hard toil, many reverses, little to eat. Years went by; father and mother dying; sisters marrying and settling in other homes; Oonagh left where she was. Even if she had had the inclination to look into the small dim mirror in the house she had little time. Only in the coming of young men about the place might she have known she was comely to look at. They had brought gifts, as wooers; but never could she give answering love, and by and by they had grown discouraged – who could blame them ? – and had found other girls as beautiful and not so strange. For she had strange ways. She would leave tasks in the midst and run off over the moors to the lochan. She began to say she had a lover, a husband, a home in its depths.

At last only one brother remained, and a hard life he had of it trying to keep the croft with her fitful aid. He took a dislike to the place. He had a sweetheart whose family moved to the east where farming was more rewarding. He could go there, and take his sister with him.

But when he told her of the plan, Oonagh would not hear of leaving. How could she leave her home, the trysting place, where alone she had hope of being with her lover? And perhaps in his heart her brother was not sorry to escape.

Peat cutters, Isle of Lewis (Colin McPherson)

'She has lived ever since, as you see, alone.' My mother rose to go, but I held her back.

'He never came again then, her lover?'

She paused, as if reluctant to continue the story, but at last she said, 'Yes, he did come. That was the funny thing, he did come back to her.' One day a carriage and pair was observed coming up the Brae, along the main road past Druim, to Loch Laide. It stopped where some men were working at the side of the road. A gentleman got out, dressed I suppose in old-world style, twin gold chains reposing on his stomach, one for his watch, one for his sovereign case. To the surprise of the men he put his question in Gaelic. 'Was there a family living yet in the moorland croft behind the Leitir? And a girl called Oonagh, was she married yet?' The older among them knew then who he was, and I have no doubt they left the ditch uncleared to go and spread the news. The time was come at last. That poor solitary woman, whom some shunned as unlucky because lovelorn, would get her due reward at last. There was no mistaking the eagerness on the stranger's face.

I cried out, 'Then why –?'

My mother seemed to shiver. He returned in less than an hour. This time he did not speak, but went as fast as he could away. The account of their meeting came from a child who, curious, ran over the heather and got near enough to witness the manner of it. Oonagh came to the door to receive her caller, then stopped short at seeing a stranger. He held his hands out. 'Do you not remember me? I have come back as I said I would.' She stared at him bewildered, making no move towards him, no sign of recognition. 'I have never loved anyone as I could have loved you. I am home now. I will make up to you for all the years I have left you forsaken.'

'Then why? Did he not live long after coming?'

'He lived all right. He is still alive, alive and prospering. He is in business in the town. It was Oonagh who would not . . . It was as if she had never seen him before. She would not let him touch her. She said the only man she loved was in the lochan. I tell you only what you know.

'From that the story has grown that she is in love with the spirit of the lochan, or even that the *eachd uisge*, about which your father will tell you there is no such thing, has put his spell upon her. Now she is past the time of women it is easier for her. It is only now and again the idea takes hold of her. She is quiet and has done no one any harm. All the same, Ellen, if you go to her place you must not go out on the moors with her.'

I needed no forbidding. I was a timid child. I doubt if I went to the tiny croft ever again. And she never asked me. Whenever we met, at schoolhouse service or on the Druim road, she would smile from her wrinkled sunburnt face, if she were not contentedly puffing at her clay pipe. That was all.

But sometimes, when I heard the creaking sound of a cart upon a rocky road, I would be visited by a perverse longing to go with her again to her lochan and see that ecstasy I might not share.

# Busman's Holiday

LOUISE TURNER 1988

This is a story set in a Glasgow of the distant future, maybe a hundred years on from now. In 1988, the year in which this story was published, local bus services were 'deregulated' in Scotland in order to increase competitiveness. For a while, to the confusion of passengers, convoys of mainly empty, vari-coloured buses seemed to roam the streets. They were bedecked with a variety of slogans: 'Welcome aboard. We're going your way.' So although this is a story of the future, the author may be trying to tell us that her vision is not all that far-fetched.

Have you ever heard about the old days, the days when Glasgow was a city full of people? Most folks had cars then, and buses used to fill the streets. I only know because my Nan told me, and even she can't remember that far back. The sight of buses streaming up Renfield Street in the early morning sun must have been amazing, but now, as I wander Glasgow's deserted roads, I can hardly believe it.

My name's Rhona, and I'm seventeen. I'm going to be a bus-driver, and this year I'll be in my first bus-race. My Dad's a bus-driver – no, not *a* bus-driver, he's the best bus-driver in all Glasgow and, for the eighth year running, he's been picked to drive Lord Clydeside's bus in the race tomorrow. I live in a huge house in Pollokshields, with lots of grass and apple trees in the front garden. His Lordship believes that his busmen should get the best, and that's why he gave us the house.

Nan says that when she was a girl, she lived in a poxy little house in the east. That was before they all left, lured to the jobs in the south by rosy promises that drew them away. Our family hadn't the money to move away to where the jobs were two-a-penny, so we, like so many others, stayed. Now we don't speak to the English much, and they don't speak to us, hiding behind their wall down in the Borders. We look after ourselves okay here in Scotland, and we're doing just fine under the Bus Lords. They give us all we could need: food, work, education, medicine, everything. But it's people like us, the bus-drivers, who get the best; which isn't really surprising, as we support society itself, and I think we deserve it.

Everyone holds the busmen in respect; and, for one day every year, they get a chance to show their gratitude. That day is the day of the Bus Race, held traditionally on the afternoon of the Glasgow Fair. Everything depends on the race, because only the Bus Lord with the best driver can control Glasgow for the following year.

Drivers like my Dad tell lots of stories about the old days, when the buses of Clydeside, Kelvin and Strathclyde all tried to outdo each other in the city, fighting against their rivals to provide a cheaper and better service for the community. Eventually, so they say, the Bus Lords offered us more as everyone left, keeping in touch with England when we no longer did so. As they grew more powerful and more influential, competition between them increased, and unrest occurred in the city, with the Bus Lords all trying to take direct control. Things got a wee bit out of hand, until the Bishop intervened, and, with infinite wisdom, decreed that a race between buses should take place, and whoever picked up most people in the shortest time would rule Glasgow. All that is history. Now we don't bother with the passengers (to tell you the truth, hardly anyone in Glasgow has even sat in a bus), but the race has remained the same, getting faster and more furious with every passing year. The entire city turns out to watch it, and the day has been declared a national holiday in honour of the busmen.

I hear the sound of hooves outside, and I run to the great glass door. Dad's back, leading our pony round to the grass behind the house. No one could ever wish for a better Dad than mine. He's tall and dark, and he wears a smart navy-blue uniform. He always looks proud, because he drives the Red-and-Yellow buses, and he knows they're the best. He knows he's the best, too. I run to meet him, and he turns to me, smiling.

'Well?' I ask.

'We'll win,' he says confidently. 'I was talking to Tom, mind, and he isnae driving for Lord Strathclyde this year. He's been training his Lordship's son, and the lad's bloody guid.'

'Not as good as you.'

'Och, Rhona. An old dog cannae keep its bone forever, you know. Maybe the Lord'll think it's time for someone else to lead us for a while.'

'Can I still come?'

'Aye, but you'd better not be sick. I'd never live it down!'

'I won't let you down, Dad.'

We go into the house, and sit down to dinner; beef from Renfrewshire, with carrots and tatties too, and elderberry wine from His Lordship's estate in Kilmacolm. It's worth a fortune, but Dad doesn't have to pay a thing, getting it all free in return for his services as a busman.

That night, before I go to bed, I pray and pray. I pray to God that we can win again, so that Lord Clydeside can guide our city for another year. I can scarcely get to sleep, excitement at the knowledge that tomorrow will surely be the happiest day of my life making me toss and turn restlessly. At last, though, I feel myself drift away . . .

. . . and then it is morning, and the sun blazes in through my window. I glance at the little clock on my bedside table, and it says five o'clock. I feel good, and somehow I know that we'll win. Sparrows are twittering on the roof outside as I get up and have a long relaxing bath, knowing that today I must look my very best. Then I get dressed, wearing my special clothes: a skirt of darkest navy with a lighter blouse, made of real cotton, and given to me by Lord Clydeside himself. I brush my hair, feeling every long strand spring to shining life. At last I am ready, and I go downstairs.

Dad is already in the kitchen, wearing his neatest uniform. He hands me a plate of bacon and egg, and we sit down to eat. I can scarcely eat a thing, and Nan fusses over me, scolding me for being so silly. Dad just laughs, and says he was exactly like that before his first race.

At six o' clock we leave for Paisley, our pony trotting briskly along over-grown roads, red-and-yellow cart gleaming. Dad urges her on, fire glowing in his grey eyes, the fire that only a natural busman knows. He's always been a talented driver, but he never raced until Mum died. She used to be an engineer, but she was killed in the crash of '63, and after that, Dad changed. He took to the racing, and now it's in his blood.

By eight o'clock we've reached Paisley, and turned our pony out in a field near the depot. I can see Dad's bus outside, engineers washing it down in preparation for the race, and topping up its fuel. Don't ask me where the fuel comes from. Nan thinks that Lord Clydeside owns a little oilfield down in the Clyde estuary, and that's how he can afford all the stuff from England, giving them oil in return. I'm sure Dad knows, but he won't say.

We pay a quick visit to the racing bus, which looms over me, as big as a house. Dad checks the engine, and then says to me, 'She looks fine to me, Rhona. Shall we go and see the old bus? It's nearly time to go, anyway.'

I feel a grin cross my face, and can hardly stop myself from breaking into a run. We hurry over to the huge shed, and there, standing in a shaft of sunlight which shines through a hole in the roof, is the old bus from London. Its engines are ticking over, filling the shed with a dim roar that makes the air quake around us. I gaze in wonder at it, staring at the vivid red-and-yellow paint, and reading the magic words, *Welcome aboard. We're going your way*, which are emblazoned along the side.

Dad ushers me into the back, and I make my way across the wooden floor, and sit at the very front, looking out over the bonnet at the activity going on outside. Dad climbs into the cab, and slips the engine into first gear. I've never been in a bus before, and here I am, sitting in the pride of the fleet. Dad turns the steering wheel, and the bus lumbers round with a thundering purr, like some ancient dragon waking in its den. We move slowly out into the sunshine, and then we're on our way; the other bus, ready for battle, following behind us. I want to sing, the controlled power of the bus beneath me making my spirit soar. And all the time the sun is beating down, turning the road ahead into a shimmering haze.

We drive through the ancient streets of Paisley, crowds gathering to watch as we pass, wishing us luck in the race ahead. We park outside Lord Clydeside's town house, the old Paisley town hall. Dad leaves his cab, and climbs up the steps to meet His Lordship. Lord Clydeside is already waiting just outside the vast doors, a bent and white-haired old man with a stick. He may be getting on now, but eyes still shine with wisdom, burning bright from his face and piercing the hearts of all who know him. He rules fairly and justly; and we, his people, love him.

He climbs slowly aboard the bus, and recognises my presence with a nod and a friendly smile. I feel myself blush with the honour of it; and Dad, returning to the cab, winks at me. Lord Clydeside climbs upstairs slowly, helped by his advisers. Then, when he is safe in his seat, his chief aide returns, and gives two sharp tugs to a cord which runs along the roof. A bell sounds loudly, ringing twice, and the bus starts off. We're on our way once more, heading for Glasgow, where the race will begin at noon.

The streets of Glasgow are swarming with people, and street vendors are selling sweets, trinkets and flags in the colours of the three Bus Lords. It is a child's paradise, but I am a child no longer, and I don't belong with those ordinary people any more. We drive through the city, waving to our followers who lean out of rickety tenement buildings and crowd along the well-worn pavements, with red-and-yellow flags in their hands.

We draw up in George Square. Lord Kelvin Scottish is already there, and his bus is on the starting line. He is leaning against his car, the only car that still works in the whole of Scotland. It is blue, and it is very sleek and elegant, with the sculpture of a silver angel rearing at its bonnet. With him is his driver, an old hand like Dad, who knows the set route like the back of his hand. Lord Clydeside comes carefully down the narrow staircase, and joins Lord Kelvin Scottish with my father at his side. Our bus is manoeuvred over to a space beside the Kelvin one, and I go over to it, and take my place at the front along with the engineers and the other drivers.

I stare out of the window, and at last Lord Strathclyde arrives, in a black coach drawn by four magnificent black horses, orange ribbons braided in their manes and tails, and orange lines highlighting the glossy black panels. His bus comes too, painted boldly in the same colours. Lord Strathclyde steps out, and with him is his son: blond, not much older than me, and not bad looking. He might be good, but he'll never be as good as Dad.

I wait in excitement as the vows are taken. It's quite simple. There must be no bloodshed, no sabotage, and may the best driver win. The drivers shake hands, then go to their buses and start up the engines.

The Bishop holds up a large sign that says 'Stop', and then, when he is ready, quickly flips it to 'Go'. All three buses lurch away, reaching top gear before turning down Buchanan Street. This is where the leader will be established for the first stage.

I bite my lip, knowing that Kelvin have the advantage, as they're on the inside. But suddenly Dad is ahead, feigning a swerve to the left as they reach the opening. The Kelvin bus nearly hits a tree, and Dad has got through the narrow gap, hurtling past the sculpture of the flying bird, with the orange bus close behind him.

At the bottom of Buchanan Street he cuts the corner onto Argyle Street, nearly scraping the side of the bus against a building. He is well in the lead, but the orange bus is still there and I hang on for dear life as we pass under the railway bridge.

The gap is closing; and Dad, determined to keep the lead, weaves from one side of the road to the other, the double-decker swaying dangerously as he does so. He's just ahead as we move through narrow side-streets, and then onto Sauchiehall Street, a road almost as wide as the river itself. The road cannot be blocked, so this is where buses can go as fast as the wind.

Dad jams his foot to the floor, and I can hear the engines at the rear grumbling loudly as we rattle along, the whole frame of the bus juddering in protest. We're neck and neck with the orange bus as we pass the museum, ivy clinging to a lichen-stained red building which is now as decayed as the gardens around it. I look up at the old tower of the university, standing like a sentinel amongst the ruins, and see that the Kelvin bus has made up for the ground that it lost. Then I cry out in disappointment, for – turning into Byres Road – Lord Strathclyde's son barges his way in front of us, forcing us to take evasive action. He smiles at my father, his face confident, almost complacent.

He hugs the inside all the way up University Avenue, keeping in the lead. Dad's jaw is set, and his eyes are hard, but he cannot get ahead. At the bottom of the hill, though, the orange bus slows up for the corner. Our bus flies straight past him, almost overbalancing with the tight turn, but somehow righting itself and regaining the lead. It is reckless driving like that which marks a true busman, and the younger man hasn't quite found the courage yet. The Kelvin bus swings round the corner like a veteran, closing in on the orange bus.

Our position is assured now, and I feel giddy as we pass the tall buildings of Sauchiehall Street at top speed. Dad doesn't even slow up as we reach the precinct, the bus jolting across uneven paving stones and sending over-hanging branches flying in all directions. Dad wrenches the steering-wheel round, and turns the corner at sixty miles an hour, sending the bus down Hope Street at a rate which sets my teeth on edge, and my hands are clamped tightly round the rail in front of me. I close my eyes as he takes the last two corners, barely braking as he does so.

It is only now, on the home straight, that I find the courage to look out once more. Dad is leaning forward in his seat, a manic grin on his face. The finishing tape is just ahead; and as we plough through it, Dad takes a hand from the wheel, shaking it in victory and defiance. He pulls up: and, by the time the other two finish, he is out talking to Lord Clydeside. For the sixth year running, we've won!

That evening, I sit at a long table in the City Chambers, feeling drowsy and dizzy with wine and happiness. Lord Strathclyde is making a speech, but I am hardly listening to him, as I have more important things on my mind. Lord Clydeside in his victory speech announced that my father is to be his successor as Bus Lord, which took Dad by just as much surprise as it took everyone else. And next year, I am to start my formal training as a bus driver, now I have finished school. Lord Clydeside told me that if I was half as good as Dad, I'd be a driver to be proud of. So now I am a real part of this world, and, as I look around me, I know I wouldn't swap it for anything.

# Glossary

Arranged by story in the sequence in which the words appear.

### Tartan

| | |
|---|---|
| cairn | heap of stones, found on hilltops and elsewhere, sometimes in the form of a memorial |
| plaided men | probably a reference to early versions of the kilt, worn by the indigenous inhabitants of Scotland |
| Gaelic men | speakers of Gaelic, the language of the Highlands and Western Isles |
| Byzantine coin | the Vikings reached Byzantium (modern Istanbul) via Muscovy (modern Moscow), sailing their ships down the Volga River and into the Black Sea. They brought Byzantine coins and other artefacts back to Scandinavia with them, and hence to Orkney and Shetland. |
| trull | trollop, slatternly woman |

### The Duke

| | |
|---|---|
| The Castle | Dunrobin Castle, just north of Golspie, on the east coast of Sutherland |
| Dundreary whiskers | long side whiskers without a beard, a style favoured by men in the 1850s. Taken from the name of a character in a stage play who sported this arrangement with his facial hair. |
| clarsach | Gaelic harp |
| Stafford House | London mansion of the Dukes of Sutherland |
| wethers | castrated male lambs |

### The Bridge

| | |
|---|---|
| Titch | popular nickname for a small boy. Something 'titchy' is very small. |
| 'juice' | probably lemonade |
| reeshling | rustling, crashing |

## The Old Man and the Trout

| | |
|---|---|
| spate | river in flood, especially after heavy rain |

## Clay

| | |
|---|---|
| syne | then |
| bit bairn | small baby; 'bit' is a general term of semi-disparagement |
| unco | very |
| close up | close ranks (against outsiders) |
| toun | hamlet, as in fermtoun, fishertoun, mil(l)toun, etc. |
| bit farm | small farm |
| rive up | break up, cultivate |
| flit | move house |
| swede | turnip |
| rouped | evicted, defeated |
| childe | lad, young man (The correct Scots spelling is 'chiel'.) |
| laid cannily by | put carefully aside |
| lightsome | carefree, cheerful |
| aye | always |
| parks | lands |
| mouser | moustache |
| brae | hill, slope |
| gentry | of good birth |
| faith | goodness! (an exclamation) |
| quean | girl, lassie (also 'quine') |
| losh | gosh, goodness! (an exclamation) |
| blithe | bright, happy |
| tailer | hand turnip cutter |
| hoots | nonsense! (an exclamation) |
| chave | struggle, work hard (also 'tyauve') |
| muck out the byre | clean out the cowshed |
| wynds | lanes |
| meikle roan | big roan-coloured (brown and white) horse |
| peesies | peewits, or lapwings |
| wheep | the call of the lapwing |
| britchins | breeching straps for a shaft horse |
| swiveltrees | cross-bar of a plough |

| | |
|---|---|
| swink | work |
| move canny | go carefully |
| bothy billies | young farm labourers |
| bents | moors, perhaps covered in bent, or coarse grass |
| wheeber | whistle |
| rig | strip of ploughed land |
| marts | markets |
| puddock-hunt | frog-hunt |
| whins | common gorse, or furze |
| deave | nuisance |
| kittle up daft | act up as if stupid |
| stite | mad |
| prig | entice, haggle |
| ganting | stuttering, blethering |
| hirpling | limping |
| habber | blether |
| tares | vetch plants |
| tinks | tinkers |
| pleitering | dabbling, rummaging |
| ley | lea, or unhilled field |
| greet | cry, weep |
| fettle | good condition |
| hove | raised |
| merk | penny (of profit) |
| biggings | sheds, out-houses, barns |
| coddled | spoiled, coaxed |
| gleyed | peered, frowned |
| stepping | going |
| came ben | came through (into the kitchen) |
| fee'd | apprenticed |
| lowe | flame |
| all in a fash | angry, worked up |
| coling | arranging hay in haycocks |
| breeks | trousers |
| yavil | name of the second year of the same crop of oats |
| birn | burden |
| trauchle | drudgery, work |

| | |
|---|---|
| schlorich | mess |
| nieve | grip, grasp |
| tirred | stripped, undressed |
| fairly | carefully |
| rickle | handful |
| heuch | arrow (also spelt 'heuk') |
| eirde | earth-house (should be 'eird-house', an Iron Age dwelling) |
| crack | chat, conversation |
| hoast | cough |
| gley | glance |

## The Kitten

| | |
|---|---|
| ower mony | too many |
| burn | stream, small river |
| peat-reek | smell of a burning peat-fire |

## Touch and Go!

| | |
|---|---|
| mither | mother |
| croft | upland smallholding, a small subsistence farm |
| howe | vale, valley |
| drappie | drop |
| bree | broth, soup |
| nicht | night |
| ane | one |
| jalouse | guess, suspect (pronounced 'ja-looze', emphasising the second syllable) |
| a' richt, wifie | all right, woman |
| ferlies | strange sights, spirits, fairies |
| dominie | schoolmaster (straight from the Latin 'dominus') |
| loon | boy |
| box-bed | bed set within an alcove for warmth and privacy, a common arrangement before the 20th century |
| hoose | house |
| buckie | snail |
| oxter | armpit |
| sharn midden | dung-heap |

| | |
|---|---|
| bobby | policeman |
| snibbed | dropped |
| ken | know |
| 'cheese-cutter' cap | flat cap of Edwardian style |
| putteed leg | leg encased in puttees or military leggings, like jodhpurs; formerly part of a policeman's uniform |
| crater | creature, person |
| breeks | trousers |
| girdle | flat iron pan for cooking, for example, pancakes (sometimes 'griddle') |
| gin | if |
| gweed-he'rtet | good-hearted, good-natured |
| gweed nicht | goodnight |
| myowt | whisper of protest |

## A Matter of Behaviour

| | |
|---|---|
| wee | little |
| kale | cabbage |
| away in the west | in some remote west-coast or Hebridean village |
| wifie | woman (a mainly affectionate term) |
| safe in the kirk-yard | dead and buried |
| fou drunk | very drunk |
| Corby | English new town, in Northamptonshire. Many Scots migrated to its steelworks for employment in the 1960s. |
| griddle | flat iron pan for cooking, for example, pancakes (sometimes 'girdle') |
| yards | shipyards |
| in a terrible taking | very distressed or upset |

## The Face

| | |
|---|---|
| pieces | sandwiches |
| bunnet | flat cap |
| bogeys | this word is used punningly for two meanings: (1) a sort of railway track; (2) spirits (the Bogey Man – another name for the Devil – was what generations of bad children were once threatened with in Scotland) |

## A Couple of Old Bigots

| | |
|---|---|
| darg | duty, dull routine |
| blethering | chattering |
| gawked | stared |
| pickling | getting ready to happen |
| on his hunkers | squatting down, crouching on his haunches. Protestants in Scotland often make critical reference to Catholics praying on their hunkers, in other words, kneeling down. Protestants usually pray in a seated position. |
| thae beads | those beads, in other words, Rosary beads used by Roman Catholics |
| brusher | in mining, the brusher had to brush away loose rock or coal to ensure that it did not fall on people working at the face |
| drawer | in mining, the drawer had to pull coal and rock away from the face |
| Orangeman | member of the Orange Order, a closed Irish Protestant society for the defence of the Protestant religion and the British link |
| crabbit | cross, ill-tempered |
| take a cord | hold one of the ceremonial cords attached to the four corners of a coffin when it is about to be lowered into the ground. These are customarily held by the immediate family of the deceased person, or by very intimate friends. |

## The Bit about Growing

| | |
|---|---|
| grilse | name given to a young salmon in its first year back at the spawning ground. Used here as a nickname |
| horsey | wooden trestle used in sawing wood |
| girny | ill-tempered |
| The Beano | title of a famous comic beloved of generations of youngsters |
| Standard grades | school exam usually sat by pupils aged fifteen or sixteen |
| gowk | fool; cuckoo |

| | |
|---|---|
| Doc Martens | brand name of a popular shoe or boot |
| croon | sing softly |
| carnhar | salmon fisher (a Gaelic word) |

## Christian Endeavour

| | |
|---|---|
| bandy hope/<br>  Band a Hope | Band of Hope, a Protestant evangelical hymn-singing<br>organisation |
| mind yer heid | watch your head: an ironical taunt against self-<br>importance |
| big snotter | big sniveller. A common term of contempt, the<br>precise definition of 'snotter' is 'nasal mucus'. |
| tae | to |
| fae | from |
| midden-bin | dustbin |
| close | passageway in a tenement |

## The Cure

| | |
|---|---|
| beamer of a riddy | blush, a beaming red face |
| gie's a brekk | give us a break |
| scoosh | dawdle, cinch |
| toty wee splash | tiny taste |
| smarming | acting obsequiously, sucking up |
| gaun | going |
| skives | lazes about |
| girning | moaning, complaining |
| birl | whirl around |
| skelped | smacked |
| skliffing | shuffling |
| peching | panting |
| wan | one |
| mibbe | maybe |

## Away in Airdrie

| | |
|---|---|
| gaffer | boss |
| yin | one |
| Hampden | Glasgow's huge international football stadium |
| wee box of a Stand | diminutive area providing covered seating |
| bovril | hot beef-flavoured drink, popular in cold weather |

## The Man in the Boat

| | |
|---|---|
| laird | landowner |
| awa | away |
| Black Art | magic, the devil's work. The devil was often referred to as 'the black man'. |
| ceilidh | Gaelic name for a social gathering, often involving dance, music, songs, storytelling, and other entertainment |
| sowens | a type of porridge |
| soor | sour |
| pappies | breasts |
| claes | clothes |
| coo shairn | cow dung |
| whit's adae | what's wrong |
| pit a glamourie ower him | cast a spell over him |

## The Man in the Lochan

| | |
|---|---|
| croft | upland smallholding found especially in the Highlands and Islands |
| single tutelary rowan tree | one rowan tree often guarded a house or cottage door. There was a belief that it kept evil spirits away, thus protecting the occupants of the house. |
| singling | thinning out |
| all joco | all jovial and pleased with oneself |
| m'eudail | my dear (Gaelic, a term of endearment) |
| turn her peats | peats are stacked to dry, before they are used for fuel. They have to be turned during the drying process. |
| lochan | small loch |
| churning | stirring process involved in turning milk to butter or cheese |
| eachd uisge | water horse with magic powers, sprite, or kelpie (Gaelic) |

## Busman's Holiday

| | |
|---|---|
| isnae | isn't |
| tatties | potatoes |